DISPELLED

MISS PRIMM'S ACADEMY
FOR WAYWARD WITCHES: BOOK 2

CHRISTINE POPE

DISPELLED

Copyright © 2021 by Christine Pope

ISBN: 978-1-946435-47-7

Published by Dark Valentine Press

Cover design by Christian Willmanns/Taurus Colosseum

Ebook formatting by Indie Author Services

CHAPTER 1
A NEW YEAR

My boyfriend Lochlan stretched out a hand and I took it, scrambling up the bank of the stream where we'd been wandering for the past hour or so. The warm August breeze pulled a few hairs loose from the ponytail that was doing its best to keep my long hair out of the way, but I ignored the annoying strands as I tried to focus on the treacherous footing. We'd had a light rain before dawn, and the ground was just muddy enough that I knew I needed to concentrate on where I stepped.

"Doing all right?" Lochlan asked as I came to stand next to him. If possible, his coppery red hair and clear blue eyes looked even brighter than usual, thanks to the warm sun shining down on us. Luckily, he didn't seem to freckle much, but only picked up a light golden tan from being out of doors.

"Splendid," I replied.

The rest of our little group was farther upstream, our goal the stables that sheltered a dozen horses on the grounds of the academy. After spending a glorious two weeks hiking and picnicking and generally doing our best to stay outside as much as possible, we'd all decided it was at last time to go riding. There was a sign-up sheet to request horses tacked to the wall outside the office of Miss Primm, the school's headmistress, and my roommate Juno and I had filled it out on behalf of our "octet"—our good friends Helen and Celeste, as well as the boys they were seeing, Billy and Isaac, and then of course there was also my roommate Juno and her boyfriend Dev...and Lochlan and me. We'd been planning this outing for some time, but had wanted to wait until our two weeks of freedom between terms were nearly over.

Each of us carried a small lunch in our packs, since we'd decided the best way to make an entire day of it was to ride the horses to a remote spot on the property and then have our midday meal outdoors, away from all the other students. Luckily, this was fairly easy to do, since the estate where the academy was located comprised a little more than three hundred acres, offering plenty of room to spread out.

Still hand in hand, Lochlan and I forged ahead, moving toward the stables. We knew there was no chance of getting lost, not with the entire property given a small, useful enchantment to ensure that everyone there always went exactly where they needed to go.

Which was why I was less than thrilled to see my nemesis Mona McGee and her faithful shadow, Philippa Carmody, standing at the entrance to the stables, making much of the horses who waited there. With them were the sandy-haired, gangly-looking boy from Master Marco's School for Woeful Wizards that Mona had apparently begun seeing sometime during the spring, along with another boy around our age—that is, eighteen or nineteen. He had fair, curly hair and a snub nose, and appeared to be Philippa's date.

Juno and Helen and Celeste and their respective companions arrived around the same time that Lochlan and I did. A single look at the interlopers, and Juno said with a fearsome scowl, brown eyes snapping fire, "What are *you* doing here?"

Mona tossed back a lock of her inky hair. "What do you think? We're going riding."

"Oh, no, you're not—" Juno began, but

Lochlan cut in before she could go any further, obviously guessing it was probably better to let cooler heads handle the situation.

"I think there must be some sort of mistake," he said, with a friendly, disarming smile, one he used for good effect. "I know that Callie and Juno put all our names down on the sign-up sheet for today." Pausing, he glanced over at me. "You signed us up sometime last week, right?"

"Yes," I said, doing my best to follow his lead and sound neutral and good-natured. After all, getting into a row wouldn't solve our current problem. "And," I added, "I know that Misty Cantu and Louise Langford signed up for the horses we wouldn't be using. Otherwise, there would still be enough to go around."

These reasonable arguments didn't appear to hold much water with Mona, because she only lifted her chin and replied, "Well, I didn't see your names on the sheet. If there hadn't been plenty of horses available for riding today, we certainly wouldn't have bothered to come all the way out here."

A door slammed in the stable behind us, and an older woman I'd never seen before stepped out of the building. She had gray hair pulled back into a severe knot, and the lined skin of someone who spent a good deal of time outdoors in all sorts of weather. Wearing a frown, she came toward us. "What's all this noise, then?"

"Bit of a mix-up," Lochlan said with another of his disarming smiles, that single dimple I loved so much showing in one cheek. "We signed up to take the horses out, but it appears that Miss McGee here believes it's her turn."

"Well, that's easy enough to check," the strange woman said. "Miss Primm always makes sure I have a copy of each day's sign-ups. Let me go look."

She turned and headed back toward the door from which she'd emerged a moment earlier. It was a regular door, not the split kind you'd see guarding a stall, and so I guessed she must have some sort of office there. And although none of us had met her yet, since riding wasn't part of Physical Activities for first-year students, I guessed she must be Miss Early, the horseback riding instructor.

As we waited, Juno and Mona stared daggers at one another, while their respective dates did their best to look anywhere except at the two girls. Helen and Celeste and their companions waited quietly, obviously doing what they could to avoid intensifying the confrontation.

A moment later, Miss Early reappeared, a clipboard in her hand. A frown pulled at her brows, deepening the lines between them. "I only have

Miss McGee and Miss Carmody and their friends on the list for today," she said.

What on earth? "That's not possible," I protested. "I remember very clearly putting us all down for Monday, August thirtieth. Callie Dobkins, Juno Hightower, Celeste Saint-Michel, Helen Jenkins, and all our plus-ones."

"That's not what this paper says," Miss Early told me. "Come and see for yourself."

Doing my best to ignore Juno's angry stare and the expressions of increasing puzzlement on the rest of my friends' faces, I went over to the riding instructor and stared down at the clipboard she held. Sure enough, there were both Mona's and Philippa's names—with "plus one" scribbled next to each of them—but absolutely no sign of the names I'd so carefully written on the sheet a week earlier.

"I don't understand," I said slowly. "I know I signed up all of us."

"You did," Juno put in. "I watched you do it. Someone must have erased our names and put Mona's and Philippa's there instead."

"Just what are you accusing me of?" Mona demanded. She'd taken a step forward, her heavy black brows pulled together in a fearsome frown.

"Cheating, just like always," Juno shot back.

At once, Miss Early raised a hand. "Girls," she said in quelling tones. "Those are not the sort of accusations that should be thrown around without proof." She looked over at me as she added, "I am sorry, but your name simply isn't here. I can't let you take the horses when someone else who wants them and whose name is on the sign-up sheet is here instead."

Juno's eyes narrowed, and Celeste stepped forward. "What about tomorrow?" she inquired, voice calm as always. "We can come back then."

"I am very sorry," Miss Early said again. To be fair, she did appear genuinely apologetic, and sorry that she couldn't accommodate us. "But the horses are spoken for tomorrow as well. This close to the end of the holiday, everyone is wanting to ride before classes begin again."

That was precisely why we'd waited as well. Oh, and also because we'd all agreed it was probably better to wait to go riding just in case one of us had some sort of mishap. Better to be laid up when classes began than at the start of a beautiful two weeks of holiday.

Those well-laid plans appeared to have come crashing down on us, however. Because I could tell that Miss Early was not going to budge— despite looking sympathetic to our cause—I only said, "Come on, everyone. We can go have our picnic somewhere else."

Lochlan twined his fingers with mine. "Yes,

there was that meadow we wanted to explore anyway. Come along."

The two of us began to walk away from the stables. After a pause, Helen and Billy and Isaac and Celeste followed. Juno lingered for a moment, jaw jutting out at a dangerous angle, but it seemed she finally decided as well that she wouldn't get anywhere by trying to argue her case further. One last venomous glance in Mona McGee's direction, and then she and her boyfriend Dev brought up the rear of our sad little caravan.

No one spoke as Lochlan and I guided our group away from the stables. The building was ringed by several low hills, forming a naturally sheltered spot, and so it didn't take too long before we were safely out of earshot. There, Juno stopped and planted her hands on her hips.

"She *totally* cheated."

The rest of us paused. Dev looked resigned, as if he knew the best response was to let Juno say her piece rather than try to keep it bottled up.

"How could she have cheated?" Helen asked. Like the rest of us, she didn't look very happy at the sudden change in plans. Unlike Juno, however, Helen had some practice in under-standing that the world didn't always do what she wanted. "The sign-up sheet was outside Miss Primm's office, in full sight of anyone who passed by."

"I don't know," Juno replied. Her brown eyes still crackled with anger. "But I know she did *something*. That girl is a crook."

While I would generally be the first to agree there was something shady about Mona McGee— I still hadn't figured out how she'd managed to win so many of the trials in our Beginning Spells class, despite apparently having very little in the way of natural magical ability—I didn't want to be throwing around accusations without some kind of evidence to back them up. "We don't know that," I said. "It could have just been a mix-up."

"Right," Juno said. "Because you and I just totally hallucinated walking over to that sign-up sheet last week and writing down all our names."

When she put it that way....

"Look," Lochlan put in before I could respond, "this all stinks. I understand that. But we can't change what happened, so I think we should just make the best of it. Maybe we can't go riding, but it's still a beautiful day, and we're not stuck in a classroom. Let's look on the bright side of things."

"Especially since we only have a few days left before school starts up again," Dev added. "I don't know about you, but I intend to enjoy myself while I can."

And with those words, he took Juno by the hands and spun her around. At once, she started to protest, but in a giggling sort of way that told me she was all too happy to have her boyfriend there to distract her. Soon enough, we were all laughing and chattering as we hurried toward our picnic destination, determined that nothing—not even Mona McGee—could prevent us from having fun before the stress and worry of another year descended.

I'D HOPED THAT PERHAPS DURING MY SECOND year at Miss Primm's academy, I could avoid Professor Hendricks, the stern-faced witch who taught Beginning Spells. However, it seemed we were all doomed to have her as part of our lives during our entire tenure at the school, since my class schedule told me I would have her for Intermediate Spells as well—and Celeste, who was better than any of us at picking up tidbits about what loomed ahead in the school's curriculum, had learned that the professor taught Advanced Spells, too.

"But no more Focus and Meditation," she said as we all gathered in hers and Helen's room to pore over our schedules and try to figure out what our next year might look like.

"That's a bummer," Juno replied. She was sitting cross-legged on the floor, a position we'd often had to assume during the aforementioned class. "Focus and Meditation was easy."

"For you, maybe," Helen said darkly. "I just barely passed. I could never keep my thoughts from running all over the place."

I definitely had to side with Helen on that particular point. Although I'd acquitted myself well enough in the class, I still couldn't quite believe that my focus was anywhere near where it should be.

"Not to worry," Celeste told her. "We'll still have a half-hour refresher class once a week with Professor Chopra. It's just that this year, we're to have Potions and Kitchen Magic instead."

"Bet you're looking forward to that one, Callie," Juno said with a grin.

Right then, I regretted telling my roommate the story about how I'd tried to make my mother a birthday cake one year, and instead the enchanted pastry had flown around the kitchen before she and I were able to knock it out of the air and pound on it until it finally dissolved into its constituent parts. "I've got much better control over my magic since then," I said primly.

Well, it wasn't a complete lie. I actually had made some progress over the previous year, even if I wasn't anywhere near where I wanted to be in terms of controlling my magic. Thank the Source that I had two more years of schooling to get through. Certainly by then I'd be—if not a highly trained practitioner of the magical arts—at least someone who wasn't a hazard to herself and everyone around her.

"Yes, you have," Celeste agreed, obviously wanting to stave off a squabble. "As have we all. And I have no doubt that we'll learn many useful things in our new potions class."

Perhaps. I wasn't entirely sure that I wanted to spend a whole year brewing things and learning how to use magic to make sure one's soufflés didn't fall. True, some of my reluctance probably stemmed from the realization that I would never be the kitchen witch my mother was, and so I didn't even see any reason to try. It would be better to shine in some category she hadn't already claimed as her own. Then again, my sisters were highly skilled at illusions and transmogrification, and my brother at weather magic, and so the fields where I might be able to distinguish myself without inviting comparison to one of my siblings seemed fairly limited.

And honestly, I didn't need to shine. I just needed to do well enough that I wouldn't have to worry about being banished to Mundania, that terrible world without any magic, for all eternity.

"It'll be something new at least." Juno reached for the plate of cookies we'd smuggled up to Helen and Celeste's room and took a bite. Her expression grew more cheerful as she added, "And if we get to spend at least part of the year eating cookies like this, I'm on board."

Everyone made sounds of agreement as we converged on the cookies. After all—unlike Mona McGee—we wanted to make sure each of us got her fair share.

* * *

BECAUSE THIS WAS OUR SECOND YEAR—AND therefore we all felt worldly and jaded—we weren't nearly so anxious when we trooped into the Potions and Kitchen Magic classroom that first day of the term. It was the second class of the day; we'd gone to Working With Familiars first, which was, well, familiar, and nothing that would put us off our stride.

Rather than groups of desks facing a lectern, this new classroom had long tables equipped with sinks and a variety of beakers and flasks, while one wall was entirely filled with racks of ingredients. Off to one side were three hearths placed next to each other, presumably so there wouldn't be too much jostling when it came time to heat our various preparations over the fire.

Our new professor was a round, kind-faced woman who looked like the sort of stereotypical grandmother who might be featured on a greeting card.

"Good morning, class," she said, in a voice as sweet as her expression. "I'm Professor Cauley. Some of you might be wondering why you had to wait until your second year at Miss Primm's before you could learn about potions and various other kitchen magics. There are a variety of reasons, but foremost among them is the school of thought that potions-making is more exacting than other forms of magic, and so it is better for you to have had a year of basic magic-working under your belt before branching out into a practice that can be more mentally taxing." Professor Cauley paused there, her gaze sweeping the classroom. That gaze didn't seem to pause on me, and yet I still felt myself stiffen somewhat.

I hoped very much that she wouldn't task me the way Professor Hendricks had during the Beginning Spells final examination, when I'd been required to turn an ordinary apple into pure gold. Through sheer luck, I'd managed to acquit myself fairly well, but I wasn't fool enough to believe I could continue to pull off that sort of feat.

Seated at a table closer to the wall, Mona sent the professor a confident smile. Who knows— maybe she would also be able to do well in Potions and Kitchen Magic, since a large part of it was simply being able to follow directions, with just a little bit of magic necessary to help things along.

Or maybe she was grinning like that because she knew I was looking, and wanted to continue to rub in her triumph at the stables as much as possible. Although our little group had managed to eke out a nice enough day despite not being able to go horseback riding, we all still knew something had gone horribly wrong—a suspicion confirmed when Juno had shown me a crumpled piece of paper she'd retrieved from the trash later that same day.

"You went digging around in Miss Primm's garbage?" I'd asked, aghast but also somewhat impressed by my friend's dogged pursuit of the truth.

"I didn't have to dig," Juno replied. "It was easy enough to find."

What she'd found was a discarded sign-up sheet...the real one, with all our group's names included on it, just as she and I had remembered. It seemed obvious enough that Mona must have somehow gone in and substituted her own, just to spite us.

I'd wanted to take the incriminating piece of paper to Miss Primm, but Juno had only shaken her head at the suggestion. "Better not," she told me. "I'm going to hang on to this, just in case I need evidence that Miss McGee isn't quite the goody-two-shoes she wants everyone to think she is. After all, going to Miss Primm with this isn't going to give us that day of vacation back."

Maybe not. In the end, I'd relented...but I'd also vowed never to forget what Mona had done. Clearly, there wasn't much she'd scruple to do if it meant winning some points against me and my friends.

But now I needed to focus, because Professor Cauley had continued to speak.

"An important part of making viable potions —or a good pot of soup—is quality ingredients, and so one part of this class will cover gathering the items necessary for our various projects. In fact, that is the first order of business for today. On each table, you will find a list of ingredients, all of which can be collected from the fields and groves that surround the academy, along with cloth bags to store your specimens. Go prospecting—but be back by noon."

That said, she went over and opened the classroom door. We all looked at one another, unsure as to what we were supposed to do next. Was that it? All we had to do was gather flowers and herbs?

Apparently so, because the professor made an impatient whisking motion with her hands, gesturing toward the door, and we all hurried away from the tables where we'd congregated and went outside. At once, a rush of warm air surrounded us, and Juno grinned.

"I think I could get used to this," she said as our little group headed toward the secluded copse where we'd shared many picnic lunches with our male friends from Master Marco's School for Woeful Wizards. "Gathering nuts and twigs? Count me in!"

Helen gave a cheerful nod. "Well, I suppose at some point, we'll have to combine all this stuff to make potions or whatnot, but I do like that our first day of class isn't anything harder than this!"

I also thought it was a good way to ease us into the school year. Each of our classes was an hour and a half long, but since Professor Cauley had instructed us to be back by twelve, that meant she obviously didn't expect us to do anything except forage for the items on the list she'd provided.

"Willow bark," Celeste said, inspecting said list. I reflected it was a good thing we had someone so level-headed in our group, because in our haste to get outside, none of the rest of us had thought to grab the piece of paper from where it had been resting on our table.

"There are willow trees down by the pond," I said, recalling how the graceful trees had bent over the water the times Lochlan and I had gone that way. I wouldn't bother to mention how we'd spent a good bit of our time there kissing. At least I hadn't been so oblivious I couldn't remember what kind of trees had grown in that particular spot.

We weren't the first people on the scene, but luckily, there was plenty of willow bark to go around, since the list we'd been given only asked for three pieces. After that, we headed off in search of hawthorn berries, and after that, a clump of red nightcap mushrooms.

"I wonder what Professor Cauley wants those for," Helen said dubiously, staring at the bright little fungi as Juno dislodged them from the ground. "They're awfully poisonous."

"Does it matter?" I asked. "I'm sure they're an important component of whatever potion she wants us to make out of this stuff."

Helen raised an eyebrow. "Well, it matters if you accidentally lick your fingers after touching those. You need to make sure you wash your hands with soap and water after you're done."

Juno placed the mushrooms in one of the little cloth bags Professor Cauley had provided, then said, "You seem to know a lot about mushrooms, Helen."

An embarrassed little shrug. "My mother isn't a very good witch, but she loves her garden. She taught me all about plants and flowers."

"Well, that should be helpful," I said. "Why didn't you tell us before?"

Again, Helen lifted her shoulders. "You didn't ask. Besides, none of our first-year coursework had much to do with botanical things. For this class, though—" She paused there, her expression brightening. "I think for this class, it'll help an awful lot."

I thought it would, too. We all were much cheerier as we gathered the rest of the items on the list, managing to find even the rarer ones, thanks to Helen's insightful suggestions. In fact, we were the first group to return to the classroom, something Professor Cauley congratulated us on, even though I hadn't been aware it was a competition.

After everyone had returned to the classroom, she instructed us to put our finds in a series of cubbies located next to the shelves of ingredients. "Soon enough," she said, "we will work on our first potion using the items you located today. Nothing too complex, of course, but still, something that will, I hope, give you insight into the potion-making process. Until then, however, enjoy your first day of school!"

She sent us off to lunch after that, and we were all able to eat with good appetite. Even so, I couldn't quite stop myself from worrying about what was to come in Intermediate Spells.

I had a feeling that class wouldn't be nearly as easy—or fun—as Potions and Kitchen Magic.

CHAPTER 2
A PROMISE

Professor Hendricks' classroom looked depressingly familiar. I supposed there shouldn't have been anything terribly strange about that, considering I'd last set foot in there only two weeks earlier. Still, I knew that somewhere deep down, I'd rather been hoping it would have undergone some kind of sea change during that fortnight, something that would have made it a far friendlier place.

Logically, I knew there wasn't any real reason to feel that way about the space. It was simply a room with the ubiquitous molded plaster ceiling overhead, polished wood floors underneath, and an orderly grid of desks in between. However, I didn't know what to expect from this year. If the professor could command me to turn an apple into gold, as she had during my first-year final exam, what in the world might she expect at the end of my second year?

And yes, that final examination was months and months away. Somehow, though, that knowledge didn't make me feel any better about the situation.

Professor Hendricks entered the room after we'd all sat down. Nothing about her seemed to have materially changed; she wore the same severe black suit, had her iron-gray hair pulled back in the same knot low at the back of her neck. Again, there had been no reason for me to expect anything different from her, and yet, I thought it would have made me feel better to see some evidence of her enjoying the time off she'd been given—perhaps the hint of a summer tan, or fanciful earrings to prove she'd spent some time in a warm tropical city.

Nothing like that, of course. Perhaps the professor had allowed herself to read a few frivolous books or take a walk in a meadow, but those sorts of pastimes wouldn't necessarily provide any outward indication of the time spent doing them.

"Good afternoon, everyone," she said. "It is very good to see you all back here."

An uncomfortable silence followed that pronouncement. I somehow doubted Professor Hendricks had forgotten that one of us hadn't made it to her second year; poor Abigail Andrews had been taken away by agents of DOME—the Department of Magical Exile—once it became clear that she had flunked her final exams and therefore must be banished to Mundania. Why the professor had said such a thing, I couldn't guess, unless she'd decided that a subtle hint as to what might befall anyone who didn't apply herself this year was in order.

As if any of us could forget what the consequences of failure would be.

"This year," she continued, obviously choosing to ignore the strained pause which had followed her previous statement, "we will continue to focus on strengthening your spell work and giving you the tools you will need to keep control of your magic and make it work for you, rather than vice versa. Much of this will be familiar to you, as it is more a question of reinforcing what you already know rather than acquiring new skills. Any questions?"

Her gaze landed squarely on Juno as she made that inquiry, since my friend was generally the first to have her hand in the air on any point that required clarification. This time, though, it seemed as if Juno had decided it was better to remain quiet...at least for the time being.

Possibly I was imagining things, but I got the distinct impression that Professor Hendricks was relieved by Juno's lack of a response. She went on,

"Some of you may be glad to hear that I have decided to continue our monthly trials for extra credit this year. The first one will be at the end of September. That should give you plenty of time to prepare yourselves mentally."

I forced myself not to groan, even as a nervous rustle swept through the classroom. Although I'd had no reason to believe the professor wouldn't hold those special end-of-month tests during our second year, some part of me had been hoping she might abandon them.

And I certainly wouldn't allow myself to look over at Mona McGee. No doubt she was thrilled by this development, considering that she and her team had won the lion's share of the competitions the previous year.

Juno made a low grumbling sound under her breath, and Celeste and Helen both shifted in their seats but otherwise didn't react. Clearly, none of us were too happy about having to be put through our paces all over again…only to have Mona snatch victory away from us once more.

But perhaps I was being too pessimistic. Yes, Mona and her team had won most of the trials our first year, but they hadn't won them all. There was always the hope that this time around, their percentage of wins would be even lower.

After her introduction, Professor Hendricks called up several people to demonstrate their power of illusion—Celeste to change the color of her hair, and Philippa Carmody to make it look as though clouds were floating across the classroom ceiling. Neither one of those spells was particularly difficult, and both girls did well, although Philippa's clouds were wavery enough that they looked almost like ripples on the surface of the ocean rather than full-blown cumulus billows. Even so, the professor seemed pleased, and I had the feeling that she had mainly wanted to make sure we hadn't allowed the little magic we'd learned the previous year to slip away during our two weeks of holiday indolence.

No doubt the tasks she'd devise for us after that would be considerably more difficult.

* * *

THAT NIGHT AT DINNER, MISS PRIMM ROSE TO make her usual beginning-of-term announcement and greeting. My friends and I sat at our regular table, but it wasn't completely business as usual, if only because we were now seconds, and a batch of new first-year students had replaced the girls who'd managed to successfully graduate and move on to lives as productive members of magical society.

After she was done welcoming everyone, however, the headmistress went on to say, "Those of you who are new to us this year will be happy to hear that we are continuing the relationship we began with Master Marco's School for Woeful Wizards last year. There will be various dances and other get-togethers during the coming months. The first of these will be a Harvest Ball held the last Saturday of this month. Because our final event last year was held here at our academy, the Harvest Ball will be hosted at Master Marco's school. As before, if you need to reach out to your families to request new party dresses, the staff here completely understands."

Miss Primm was smiling as she spoke; no doubt she recalled all too well the flurry of panicked letters that had gone home the year before after everyone learned that we would need more than the plain shirts and jeans and jumpers we'd packed in preparation for our time at the academy.

I realized I would need to ask my mother to send me something this time. Juno had been nice enough to get a new party dress for me for the Midsummer dance, but I knew I couldn't keep depending on her generosity. It wasn't as though my family couldn't afford to send me a whole wardrobe full of dresses if necessary—I just hadn't wanted to make too much out of all the social events Miss Primm had added to the calendar, mostly because I feared that my mother might start asking questions as to whether this new social whirl was interfering with my studies.

The headmistress concluded her speech by saying she was very happy to see all these new, eager faces in the crowd, and then she resumed her seat. An excited buzz swept over the assembled students as everyone began talking about her announcement.

"More dances and parties," Helen sighed. "I think I could quite get used to this."

"As long as it's not too much of a distraction," Celeste said as she reached for her water glass, and Juno sent her an annoyed glance.

"It's not a 'distraction,'" she said. "It's a way for us to blow off steam. There's such a thing as too much studying, you know."

"Is there?" Celeste returned with a curl of her lip. "I'm not sure how much you would know about that."

"Play nice, the two of you," I said. Juno and Celeste often went back and forth like this, but I didn't see any reason to allow the conversation to devolve into a quarrel. "It's our first day."

"First day of term," Juno corrected me. "You can't really call it our actual first day, not when we've been here for a year already."

True enough. It was still hard for me to believe that we'd known one another for a year now, that we'd spent so much time at Miss Primm's away from our families. Somehow, the life I'd lived before coming here to the academy was already beginning to feel hazy and faint, as if my quiet existence in the country house where I'd grown up was something I'd read about in a book, or which had happened to someone else altogether. Perhaps that was the point; we needed to divorce ourselves from our pasts in order to focus on the future.

A future that appeared to include at least one get-together a month with the boys from Master Marco's school. I certainly wasn't going to argue with such an arrangement, not when I was already missing Lochlan. Those two weeks of holiday when we'd been constantly in one another's company had definitely spoiled me.

Since the Harvest Ball was coming up in less than a month, I knew I had to write to my mother right away. That was why, after dinner that same night, I composed a quick note to let her know something of what to expect this coming school year.

Hello, Mother.

I hope this letter finds you well. It seems that Miss Primm has a busy social calendar planned for us this year in addition to our regular coursework, and so I think I will need several more party dresses, just to be safe. The first one is for a harvest dance, so possibly something in gold or green?

We will be studying Potions and Kitchen Magic this year. If you have any insights or tips, I would love to hear them!

Love, Callie

This missive went out with a batch of others, since I definitely wasn't the only person who'd decided to get a jump on things by writing to her family right away. And, even though my mother might have had her reservations about the number of social events that were apparently to take place during my second year at Miss Primm's, she responded by sending me not two, but three new dresses, one a shimmering blush-gold color that would be perfect for the Harvest Ball, along with a wine-colored velvet for Midwinter and a soft blue one for any spring events.

Included with the parcel that contained my new dresses was a letter from my mother.

Dear Callie,

Here are the dresses you asked for. I hope they will be suitable for the parties and dances you mentioned. I enjoyed selecting them for you—the only thing that would have made the task more enjoyable would have been to take you shopping with me. But we can look forward to that sort of expedition after you graduate.

I paused there. It was so like my mother to gloss over the fact that I had two more years of school—and the dreaded final examinations—

before I would be free to go shopping…or do anything else in the outside world. In her mind, she was thinking ahead to the future because she didn't want to contemplate what the present might be like if I failed.

Anyway, Holly is already deep in plans for her wedding, although she and Marcus have set the date for September two years from now. She wants to make sure her little sister can attend—and be part of the bridal party. We're all looking forward so much to seeing you again.

Love,

Mother

I set down the letter, frowning. Juno, who'd been lying on her bed and pretending to study, abandoned all pretense of work and sat up.

"What's the matter? Don't you like the dresses your mother sent?"

"No," I replied at once. "They're lovely. It's just that…." I let the words trail off, and allowed myself a sigh. While I appreciated my family's faith in me, I couldn't help worrying that it was entirely misplaced. What if my sister went to all the trouble of postponing her wedding until after my assumed graduation date, only to have me fail and get sent to Mundania after all?

"Just what?" Juno prompted me.

I explained about the wedding, then added,

"It's just that now I feel as though I'll have even more pressure put on me to do well here."

For a moment, Juno didn't reply. She reached under the bed and pulled out a small cardboard box, then lifted the lid and extracted a cookie. "Want one?"

Of course I did. I got up from my own bed where I'd been sitting, and went over and took a cookie. They were some of Miss Greenbriar's famous ginger-molasses cookies, sweet and chewy and utterly decadent. Technically, we girls weren't supposed to have food in our rooms, but since no one really checked, that rule was broken frequently.

As I sat there and chewed, Juno said, "I think it's really nice of your sister to wait to get married until you're done with this place. How would it have felt if she'd gone ahead and had the wedding without you?"

I didn't have to think about that question for very long. "It wouldn't have felt very good," I admitted.

"Well, then," Juno responded as she reached for another cookie. "Honestly, you were already putting plenty of pressure on yourself. But you did fab on your exams last year, and there's no reason to think you won't do the same thing this year. Stop worrying and eat your cookie."

This admonishment made me smile, as I knew

she'd hoped it would. Obediently, I took another bite of ginger-molasses, and thought how lucky I was to have Juno as a friend.

She made everything seem effortless…even when I knew it really wasn't.

BECAUSE THE WEATHER REMAINED FINE, Professor Cauley continued to send us out to forage for the ingredients we might need for our potions or other kitchen magic. In fact, we spent so much time gathering roots and herbs and leaves over those first few weeks of our second term at the academy that we had yet to concoct a single elixir.

"It seems like a waste of our time," Helen complained one fine Thursday morning while we were out on yet another of these expeditions, with only a few days to go until the Harvest Ball. "After all, once we're back in the real world, we can buy all these things at the apothecary."

Juno tilted her head, setting her fine, springy curls bouncing. "Quit griping. Isn't it better to be out wandering around the countryside than stuck in a classroom? I'm sure when January rolls back around, you'll feel different about the whole situation."

Apparently, Helen hadn't thought about it

that way. She set the basket she'd been carrying down on a tree stump and pursed her lips. "Well, maybe. But still, if we don't start learning some potions soon, I'm worried that we won't be taught enough to do well on the exams."

"Professor Cauley isn't going to test us on anything that wasn't covered in class," Celeste said reasonably. As usual, there wasn't a hair out of place in the sleek ponytail she wore, despite the way we'd been tromping along next to a stream for the past half hour. That day, we'd been tasked with gathering water plants, and so our baskets were filled with watercress and duckweed and sneezewort. "That wouldn't be fair."

"Since when does 'fair' have anything to do with it?" Juno remarked. "I mean, I don't think it's fair that we have to jump through all these hoops just to stay in the world where we were born, but no one asked me."

Since much the same thought had passed through my mind on more than one occasion, I didn't bother to argue. "I'm sure it will be fine," I said mildly. "And Juno's right—I'd much rather be out here in the fresh air for as long as the weather holds. We can sit inside and brew potions all winter, you know."

Right then, we heard voices approaching— Mona McGee and her little gang. Since we'd done a pretty good job so far of avoiding Mona when we were out in the wild, so to speak, we all fell silent, picked up our baskets, and hurried upstream. A few moments later, we paused again, confident that we'd left the troublemakers behind.

"Ugh," Juno said, once we'd determined we were alone once more. "There are a whole lot of reasons why I'll be glad to be done with this place, but never having to see or hear Mona McGee ever again has got to be one of the biggies."

We all nodded. However, Helen's expression turned thoughtful, and she said, "And what about all of us?"

"What about us?" Juno returned, brow wrinkling slightly.

I thought I understood what Helen was asking. "I'm sure we'll find a way to see each other after we graduate. It's not like being banished—we'll be free to do whatever we like."

"In our own countries," Helen said. "I mean, it'll be easy for you and me, Callie, since we're both from England, but—"

"France is only across the Channel," Celeste broke in. "It will certainly be a simple thing for me to come visit here…although I think it would be much more fun to all meet in Paris."

Juno's eyes lit up. "Oh, that sounds like an awesome idea. I can travel wherever I want, so going to France isn't a big deal. Let's all promise to meet in Paris on the one-year anniversary of our graduation. We can go shopping and drink champagne."

Those definitely sounded like worthwhile pursuits. I'd never had champagne—or any kind of alcohol, except some hard cider—and sitting in a café in Paris and drinking champagne with my friends sounded like the height of worldliness.

"It's a plan," I said. "Let's all swear on it."

We locked pinkies and solemnly promised to meet in Paris a year after our graduation. When we were done, we all looked at one another, feeling a bit awkward. It might have been a vow we'd come up with on the fly, so to speak, and yet I thought we all could tell that we'd put something powerful in motion. It wasn't quite the same thing as casting a spell, but we knew this was a promise we wouldn't break.

Now the only thing to do was succeed so we really could make that trip to Paris two years in the future.

CHAPTER 3
SOCIAL CLIMB

It was like one of those dreams where you did the same thing over and over again, always expecting something different to happen, even though it never did.

In this case, though, I wasn't dreaming. No, I was standing at the front of Professor Hendricks' classroom, getting ready to put myself through another trial.

And all right, the situation was slightly different in that I knew exactly why I was there, and was even a bit more confident than I would have been a year earlier. I'd made my mistakes along the way, but at least I'd been able to turn an apple into gold. Remembering that feat always helped me to focus; there was nothing more encouraging than past success.

"Very well, Miss Dobkins," Professor

Hendricks said. "It is your turn to create the illusion. Make it look as though the sun is coming up
in this classroom."

I swallowed. Honestly, I'd wanted Juno to
represent our team during this trial, since she
tended to be better at illusions than I was. But
she'd protested and said there was too much room
to fail spectacularly, and she didn't want to be
responsible in case the situation spiraled out of
control.

With the subtext being, I suppose, that it was
better for me to cause an unmitigated disaster. For
some reason, all three of my friends seemed to
think that my excellent end-of-term score after
our first year had made me untouchable. I really
didn't know why they continued to harbor such a
belief, since neither Professor Hendricks nor any
of our other professors had informed us that our
scores from the previous year would carry over to
the next. We'd all started our second year with a
clean slate.

Since I couldn't back out—and because Mona
McGee was watching me, yet another smirk
twisting her mouth—I pulled in a breath and told
myself to focus. We didn't have regular classes
with Professor Chopra this year, but we'd had one
of our weekly meditation sessions with her just
the day before.

I hoped that would be enough.

Another breath, and I did my best to fix a picture in my mind of what I had experienced the few times I was actually up early enough to see the sun rising—the gradual warming of the sky to the east, the quiet hush of the world just before it awoke with the dawn...the fiery disc as it seemed to melt over the horizon.

Now all I had to do was replicate those images here in the classroom. It seemed that my magic worked best when I wasn't attempting to recite a spell, and so I decided not even to try to remember the words of an applicable enchantment. Since many witches and wizards cast all their charms subvocally, my silence shouldn't be enough to arouse any suspicions.

The wall behind Professor Hendricks' desk seemed the best place to cast such an enchantment, even though it was—I thought—located to the north rather than to the east. But it was empty except for a large, rarely used blackboard, and so provided the blank canvas I needed.

I closed my eyes for a moment, thinking of how I'd seen just a faint sliver of light at first as the sun began to rise, growing brighter and brighter until I had to turn away lest that image be burned permanently on my retinas.

"Ooh...."

Since my eyes were closed, I didn't know who had breathed that syllable. I allowed myself to crack an eyelid and saw that a warm, golden flush had begun to spread across the wall, that what appeared to be bright, molten sunlight was starting to seep up from the place where the floor joined that wall. It really did look like the sun rising.

Except that no sun had ever done what that light did next.

It formed into a floating globule of searing brilliance and bounced into the air, moving toward me. As it got closer, I could actually feel the heat emanating from it, so warm that I quickly backed away. However, the floating light apparently wanted to give chase, because it followed me even as I bobbed and wove around the front of the classroom, trying in vain to keep it away.

"Is there a problem, Miss Dobkins?" inquired Professor Hendricks.

Several of the girls giggled.

"Um, no," I responded, ducking around the desk. Darn it, that thing was still on my tail.

Voice still calm and dry, the professor said, "It looks as though there's a problem, Miss Dobkins."

"Just a minute—" I began, but then had to flatten myself against the floor as the angry miniature sun I'd apparently summoned out of nowhere decided to launch itself directly at my head.

Because I was lying prone on the floorboards,

I didn't see precisely what happened next. There was a swish of a skirt and a creak of her shoes, and Professor Hendricks stood over me. While I couldn't hear her say anything, I guessed she must have invoked some sort of charm or incantation, because in the next moment, the tiny sun had disappeared.

"It's safe to get up now," she said, her tone dry.

Holding back a curse, I pushed myself to my feet. As I'd suspected, the miniature sun was gone, although my classmates were still murmuring and chuckling amongst themselves.

"I'm sorry about that, Professor Hendricks," I said. "I was only trying to conjure the illusion of a sunrise—"

"But you conjured a sun instead," she finished for me. "I would say that was a rather remarkable example of your talent asserting itself...except it's not what I asked for. You may sit down."

Cheeks burning, I resumed my seat. Helen looked worried, Celeste halfway amused, but Juno leaned toward me and whispered, "That was amazing! I've never seen anyone do something like that before."

"But it wasn't what I was supposed to do," I responded morosely. Yes, it was the first trial of the year and I'd have plenty of chances to redeem myself, but right then, I only wished I could have gotten it right. An early success would have been a good omen for the rest of the year.

As I sank against the back of my chair, I watched Professor Hendricks call on Mona McGee to perform the same illusion. Naturally, she executed the task flawlessly, earning a hundred points for her team. She shot me a triumphant smile as she sat back down, and I tried not to grind my teeth.

This was going to be a very long twelve months.

* * *

THOUGHTS OF MONA AND OUR NOT-SO-subtle rivalry were banished soon enough, however, because the Harvest Ball was being held just two days after my summoning of the minia-ture sun, and my friends and I put our energy into first anticipating the event, and then getting ready for it. As Miss Primm had told us, the dance would be held at Master Marco's school, and so a long line of shiny black cars appeared at the academy to whisk us away.

This wasn't our first rodeo, as Juno had so charmingly phrased it, and so we knew something of what to expect. Still, this night felt very different from the last dance we'd attended here at Midwinter, as the night air was still warm enough that I only needed a light wrap over the rose gold party dress I wore, and the fields on either side of the road were covered in tall grasses going to seed, rather than buried under piles of snow.

But the outlines of the large turreted building where Master Marco's school was housed were familiar enough—and so were the faces of the boys who waited for our little group as we got out of our car.

"That's quite a dress," Lochlan said after he'd given me a welcoming hug. "Where did you get it?"

"Oh, my mother bought it for me," I replied, trying not to blush too badly. While I loved the admiration in his eyes, it felt a bit overwhelming. At the same time, I uttered a thank-you to the Source that my mother had gotten me gowns that felt adult and yet entirely appropriate, with a small bit of cleavage and nothing about them that was at all reminiscent of the frilly party frocks she'd dressed me in when I was little. "I just told her what colors I was thinking of, and she did the rest."

"Well, she did a bang-up job," Lochlan told me. "That color really suits you."

About all I could do was offer him a smile. He seemed to realize he was making me nervous, because he abandoned the compliments and asked me if I wanted to have some punch. This sounded like a wonderful idea; we headed over toward the refreshments, which was also where Helen and her date Billy had gone. True to form, Juno and Dev —and Celeste and Isaac—had moved straight for the dance floor.

I'd want to dance later, but for the moment, I was simply happy to be in Lochlan's company, since we hadn't seen each other for nearly a month at that point. I waited off to the side while he got us two cups of punch—well, cider, actually, since that was what was being served, fitting the harvest theme of the dance—and then, by unspoken agreement, we headed off toward the same balcony where we'd shared our first kiss months and months earlier.

"How's the first month of your second year gone?" he asked as he leaned up against the balustrade.

I shrugged. "Well, I haven't blown up anything yet...but I did manage to conjure a miniature sun in Intermediate Spells."

Lochlan grinned. "Was that what you intended to do?"

"What do you think?" I asked with a grimace.

His smile only widened. He leaned down and gave me a quick kiss on the cheek before saying, "Well, that's still impressive, even if it was a mistake. At least you were able to get your magic to do *something*. I was supposed to levitate a sack of potatoes from one end of the classroom to the other, and I was only able to make one potato roll out of the sack and down the floor a foot or so." A pause, and he added, "And even then, I'm not sure that wasn't just gravity, and not my magic working on the thing."

Lochlan's expression was so rueful that I couldn't help chuckling. "We are a couple of sad cases, aren't we?" I said.

"Oh, I don't know…we're both still here, aren't we?"

That was true enough. I couldn't keep myself from thinking about poor Abigail Andrews, banished to Mundania for all time.

Some sort of shadow must have crossed my face, because Lochlan asked, "What's wrong?"

For a second or two, I didn't reply. Then I said, "How do you think they do it?"

"Do what?" he responded, looking mystified.

"Take people to Mundania. That is, I know the people at DOME use their magic to open up a portal between the worlds somehow, but how does it really even work? They erase the memories of the people who are exiled, but do they give them memories to replace the ones they've stolen? How else could anyone function there?"

Lochlan took my hands; I'd set my cup of punch down on the balustrade a moment earlier.

Voice gentle, he said, "Are you sure you should be worrying about this right now?"

Probably not. I'd come to the dance to see my boyfriend and have fun, not worry about what happened to those poor unfortunates who were banished by DOME. Unfortunately, my brain didn't seem eager to let the matter go.

"I'm not worrying," I replied. "I'm wondering. It just seems as though the people at DOME would have to give the exiles some kind of false memories, or how would they even fit in? Even in Mundania, you'd think someone would notice a bunch of people with amnesia showing up out of the blue."

"Maybe," Lochlan said, still in that same gentle tone. I could tell he was humoring me, but at least he seemed willing to go along with my wild theorizing for the time being. "They probably have spells to help people with the transition." He stopped there, blue eyes searching my face. "Your father works for DOME, doesn't he? Why don't you ask him?"

The mere thought of trying to bring up such a topic with my father made me shudder slightly. "Oh, no…I couldn't."

"Why not?"

Lochlan sounded genuinely curious. I lifted my hands in a helpless gesture. "Because…because the people at DOME never talk about their work.

Not even with their families. It's just not done. And my father especially would never discuss any of that with me."

An uneasy silence hung between us for a moment. Then Lochlan ventured, "Because you're attending Miss Primm's?"

"Yes," I said simply. There really wasn't any point in denying it, was there? Perhaps my father discussed some aspects of his work with my mother, but never in a hundred years would he contemplate talking about the mechanics of exile to Mundania with a daughter who might soon suffer that very same fate.

Once again, Lochlan was quiet. He reached out and touched my hair, but softly, as if he knew better than to tousle the carefully set curls Celeste had placed there with her magical curling iron only a few hours earlier. "Well," he said, in a very different tone of voice, "I suppose it's nothing either one of us can do much about. But what we can do is have a good time while we're here."

He was right, of course. It really was silly of me to be obsessing over banishment while I still had plenty of time to ensure I would never meet that fate.

Especially when I had come here tonight to enjoy myself.

"Then you need to show me a good time, Lochlan," I said with a sly little smile.

"I'm fairly sure I can do that."

He bent down and kissed me, the sweetness and spice of cider on his lips, and for a few minutes, I didn't think of anything much beyond how good it felt to be back in his arms.

Then I heard an ostentatious throat-clearing, and my hackles went up as I recognized Mona McGee's voice.

"Oh, I'm sorry," she drawled. "Were we interrupting something?"

Lochlan and I both gave a guilty start, and immediately backed away from each other. Standing a few feet from where we stood were Mona and the sandy-haired boy from Master Marco's school whom she'd been dating. He wore a smirk almost as unpleasant as her own.

"I told you she was a bratty little social climber," Mona said next, and I frowned.

"'Social climber'?" I repeated, not sure what she was going on about.

One black bar of an eyebrow lifted infinitesimally. "You mean he hasn't told you?"

"Told me what?" I said. I slanted a look up at Lochlan, who now appeared almost guilty. "What's she talking about?"

Mona put a hand to her mouth and let out an extremely unconvincing giggle. "Oh, I'm sorry. I just thought you must know that Lochlan is the eldest son of the Earl of Dundee. I figured that must be why you were always hanging around him." She giggled again. "Come on, Stanley. It looks like this balcony is already occupied."

The two of them turned and headed back toward the corridor, while I planted my hands on my hips and stared up at my companion. "You're the Earl of Dundee?" I demanded.

"No," Lochlan said, sounding annoyed. "The Earl of Dundee is my father."

"But you'll be the earl one day."

He pushed a hand through his copper-hued hair. "I suppose so."

"And you didn't think to tell me?"

His jaw hardened. "I didn't think it was important. It doesn't change who I am."

"Maybe not, but—"

I didn't get the chance to go any further than that, because he bent and kissed me again, stifling my protests. And honestly, I wasn't quite sure why I was so angry with him, except that I couldn't understand why he'd hidden such an important detail about himself from me.

The kiss ended, and I came up spluttering. "You need to explain yourself, Lochlan Abernathy. I can't believe we've been together for months and months, and you haven't said a single thing this whole time!"

The lighting in the room wasn't very good, but I still detected a flicker of irritation in his blue eyes. "Because it's like I said. It shouldn't have made any difference. Besides," he added, now sounding tired, "there's a very good chance I won't be the earl one day. If I can't manage to pass my coursework, I'll be banished and the title will pass to my younger brother."

Just as soon as it had come, my annoyance vanished. I reached out and took his hands, and said, "I'm sorry. I didn't mean to lose my temper."

"There's nothing to apologize for," Lochlan replied. "I know I should have said something to you. It's just...I suppose I couldn't figure out a way to say it without sounding like a pompous ass. You know—'oh, hello—just wanted to let you know that I'm the heir to Dundee. Toodle pip.'"

I couldn't help chuckling. "No one in Scotland says 'toodle pip.' Actually, no one in England says that, either."

The worried expression he'd been wearing vanished, and he grinned down at me. "No, I suppose they don't. I just didn't want you to think I was some posh type, looking down on the commoners or something."

"You've never given me that impression," I told him. "You're one of the most down-to-earth people I've ever met."

"Some would say that isn't necessarily a compliment, but I'll take it."

Since laughter danced in his eyes, I could tell

he was teasing me. And no, I supposed in a world ruled by magic, being "down to earth" possibly wasn't a desirable trait, but I did appreciate that about Lochlan. He might have been the eldest son of an earl, but there was absolutely no pretension in him at all.

We stole a few more kisses and then headed back to the hall. I hadn't seen Miss Primm earlier, but now I spotted her standing near the musicians, with Master Marco at her side. Her gown that evening was a bit more subdued than the wine velvet dress she'd worn to the Midwinter Ball the year before, but its dark brown silk and subtle beading around the neckline were still very pretty.

And, judging by the way Master Marco kept staring at her, it seemed he was equally entranced. Once again, I found myself wondering if the two of them had spent their two-week holiday together, and, if so, where they had gone. They did seem to be getting along very well.

Lochlan must have noticed where I was looking, because he said, "Master Marco was gone the entire two weeks—he didn't show up until the night before classes were about to start. I can assume much the same thing happened with Miss Primm?"

"Exactly the same," I replied. We'd all shared speculations about whether the headmaster and headmistress had spent their holidays together, but this was the first confirmation I'd gotten that Master Marco also hadn't returned until the very last minute. "I suppose it's rather refreshing that they're not trying to hide anything."

"Why should they? They're both adults, after all."

This observation was true enough, and yet I thought the situation might be a bit more complicated than that. I didn't know what traditions ruled the headmasters of the School for Woeful Wizards, but I did know that all the previous Miss Primms had been resolutely single. There didn't seem to be much room for any kind of permanent relationship in that sort of setup.

Well, I had to assume the two of them knew what they were doing. As Lochlan had just pointed out, they were adults and could make their own decisions.

"As are we," I replied with a smile. Lochlan was two months younger than I—his birthday was in early May—and so we'd both been the ripe old age of nineteen for some time now. "Although I'll admit that sometimes it doesn't feel that way."

"Because of being in school," he agreed. "I know—it does seem as though we're stuck in limbo these days. But I know of a way to feel better about the situation."

"What's that?" I asked, although I'd already guessed what he was about to propose.

"By dancing." He held out a hand. "Let's dance some of our cares away."

That sounded like an excellent idea. I twined my fingers with his and let him lead me to the dance floor. And as he put his arms around me, the slow tempo of the music telling us we could be close for at least this one piece, I thought he'd been exactly right.

Being held by Lochlan Abernathy was the perfect way to forget my worries…if only for a few moments.

Professor Cauley moved to the front of the room and said, "I have an announcement to make."

Almost at once, I could feel myself begin to tense. At our school, announcements rarely boded well for the student body. Or at least, announcements from the professors were seldom welcome. Miss Primm's pronouncements were usually about some sort of exciting social activity, and therefore couldn't be placed in the same category.

Under her breath, Juno groaned, "Ugh, what now?"

The professor ignored the mutters that swept through the classroom. Voice brisk, she said, "One tenet of magic which is often ignored in the midst of your studies is that all magic is connected. We are studying potions and kitchen magic in this class, but your success in this course is connected to how well you learned to focus and meditate during your first year here at the academy. It is also connected to the enchantments you cast in Intermediate Spells, because your successes and failures there—or in Working With Familiars—can translate to how well you do in my class. With that in mind, I would like to announce that our focus for the remainder of the year will be interdisciplinary magic."

I blinked, and tried to determine whether having everything connected would be a good or a bad thing. So far, I'd bumbled along all right in the potions class, although the elixir I'd concocted to make me a bit more energetic in the morning had been so over-powered that it kept me up for three nights straight before I finally collapsed and slept for nearly twenty-four hours. By sheer stupid luck, my day-long sleep had occurred over the weekend, and so I hadn't missed any classes, but still, it was not an experience I cared to repeat.

Juno's hand shot in the air.

"Yes, Juno?" Professor Cauley said, sounding amused. Luckily, she seemed to regard Juno's constant questions as an interesting phenomenon, rather than an annoyance the way Professor Hendricks did.

"How does interdisciplinary magic work?" my friend asked. "I mean, are we going to be studying potions in Intermediate Spells and incantations here in Potions and Kitchen Magic?"

"Not exactly," the professor replied. "Think of it more as working harder to see the relationships between the different disciplines, and how the techniques you learn in one class can help you gain greater insight into another. You've already laid a great deal of the groundwork, and so now is the time to begin taking a more holistic approach to your magic."

This all sounded somewhat appealing…in theory. However, I had to wonder how well it would work in practice. Professor Cauley might be confident that we'd already put the ground-work for successful magic-working in place, but I had my doubts. So far, I'd mismanaged as many spells as I'd successfully cast.

But perhaps looking at magic as a greater whole rather than finite little bits and pieces would help me to get a better grasp on the thing. Honestly, I didn't see how it could hurt.

And it did seem that a new perspective as we started a new year might also be beneficial. Autumn had whizzed by, and with it that year's Midwinter celebrations. Now they were behind us, and the coming of spring only six weeks away. Soon enough, summer would be upon us.

Well, not that soon, luckily. I was looking forward to warmer weather, just as everyone else was, and yet I knew we still had a great deal to learn in the time that remained during our second year at the academy.

This novel approach to magic was put to the test almost immediately, for Professor Cauley instructed us to concoct a potion using various herbs and roots we'd gathered in the autumn before the weather turned cold and dank...but to have our familiars be the ones to actually bring us the herbs in the correct order.

"For you know," she continued, "that potion-making can be a time-consuming and complicated affair, and having your familiars help will allow you to focus on your stirring technique, as well as maintaining concentration so the enchantments are fixed to the ingredients as required."

Her instructions made sense, because I'd botched more than one potion by getting so flustered at the prospect of assembling my ingredients and adding them in the proper sequence that my concentration was thoroughly shot. And if there was one thing most of my instructors would agree on, it was that I did have a very good rapport with my two familiars.

Others in the class didn't appear quite so pleased by this new arrangement. Mona McGee in particular was looking like a thundercloud, her heavy brows drawn together in annoyance. The passage of time didn't seem to have improved her relationship with her rat familiar very much; Silas rarely obeyed her commands, causing her to fail almost every familiar-based trial or test she took.

But it seemed she wasn't ready to argue the merits of interdisciplinary magic that involved working with familiars with Professor Cauley, because she only took her place at the worktable she shared with Philippa Carmody and waited, Silas sitting on her shoulder and pointing his long, sharp nose in the air.

The rest of us took our own positions as well. Everyone looked anxious, even those of us who worked well with our familiars. The professor might have claimed that adopting an interdisciplinary approach to our magic would serve us well in the end, but I could tell that none of my classmates were feeling too sanguine at the moment.

Professor Cauley didn't appear put off by the glum faces around her. No, she offered us a smile that lit up her plump features and said, "We'll start with something simple. Please create a potion for ensuring clear skin."

A few years ago, I'd used such a potion, one made by my mother. Taking it faithfully every morning for six months had ensured that my troublesome adolescent skin would bother me no more.

Now I had to hope I'd be able to duplicate her success.

Because I'd used such a potion before—and because we'd covered the basics of such a concoction just a week earlier—I thought it should be fairly simple. Each of us had a cubby on one side of the classroom/laboratory where we stored all the various supplies we'd gathered during the fall. I thought of the ingredients I would need—dandelion root, and milkweed, and fresh leaves of spearmint. I visualized all those items and sent Flotsam and Jetsam to gather the things I required, then went ahead and filled a glass bowl with fresh water from the tap.

All around me, my classmates were doing much the same thing. Or at least, they were getting water while their familiars went off to collect the rest of the necessary supplies. Even Mona's rat Silas seemed to have figured out what he needed to do, because he'd hurried off toward her cubby, tail twitching.

This wasn't a race, but I was still heartened to see Flo and Sam return with their ingredients before any of the other familiars had gotten back to their respective mistresses. I offered them a smile and a silent thank-you, then began stirring the items one by one into the bowl of clear water before me.

By that point, there was no need to cook a

potion over the fire; Professor Cauley had taught us how to use our magic to heat water to the correct temperature without needing a stove or a hearth. True, we'd all managed to bungle this trick as we learned our way through it, either heating the water too much or not enough, but now, nearly six months into the class, even I could manage well enough.

The other trick was to stir in the correct direction—clockwise as the dandelion root was added, the opposite way for the spearmint leaves—and to keep stirring until exactly the correct amount of thickening occurred. My potion began to grow more viscous, and to show glimmers of iridescence along its surface.

Perfect. Or at least, it looked perfect. The true test would be once I had to take it. Not that my skin wasn't good now, but a botched potion generally would have the opposite effect from what was desired...an effect that would be almost immediate, unfortunately.

Next to me, Juno stirred away as well, her brow furrowed in concentration. Fred was perched on her shoulder, offering encouragement, although I somehow doubted that his squawks of, "Stir, baby, stir!" were exactly what she needed right then.

"Five more minutes," Professor Cauley said.

Luckily, my potion was already exactly where I

wanted it to be. Stirring it further would only
cause it to congeal and lose potency, so I set down
my wooden spoon and waited. Flo and Sam had
taken up refuge in my cardigan pockets once
they'd completed their task of bringing me the
necessary ingredients, which meant all of us had
very little to do during those last few minutes.

"And time," said the professor. "Let us see how
you all did. Philippa?"

Poor Philippa did have a tendency to break
out in spots whenever she was stressed, so I could
see why Professor Cauley would have chosen her
to go first. It would be almost immediately
apparent whether she'd been successful at
concocting her potion.

With a hand that shook a little, Philippa
picked up a ladle and scooped up a decent-sized
measure of her potion. Just the briefest pause, and
then she took a large swallow.

That morning, she'd been sporting a bright red
spot almost in the direct center of her forehead.
As we all watched, the spot shrank down to nothing. At the same time, her skin overall became
brighter and clearer, almost as if it had its own
inner glow. She looked happy and fresh, and as
though she'd just come in from a brisk walk under
a friendly summer sun.

"Excellent," Professor Cauley said, voice warm

with approval. "You've done very well. See for yourself."

Out of nowhere, she conjured a hand mirror and gave it to Philippa, who peered into it almost fearfully, as though she didn't quite trust the professor's praise. As soon as she caught sight of her reflection, however, she let out a gasp.

"Oh, my skin looks ever so much better!" she exclaimed.

"Yes," the professor said. "That is a very well-executed potion. You may wish to bottle the remainder so you always have it on hand."

A bottle appeared in the professor's hand. She gave it to Philippa, who murmured a thank-you and then began to carefully fill the bottle with the remaining potion.

"Very good," Professor Cauley said. "Now you, Helen."

Poor Helen blanched, then ladled some of the potion she'd created and forced herself to take a sip. Privately, I thought Helen was certainly not in need of that particular type of concoction, because her skin was always a perfectly lovely peaches and cream.

Not in that moment, however. As soon as she swallowed the potion, her smooth complexion began to erupt in a series of extremely unfortunate spots.

"Oh, no!" she cried, dropping the ladle. "I can just feel them popping out!"

"Too much dandelion root," Professor Cauley observed. "It is so important to get the ratios correct."

"What am I supposed to do now?" wailed Helen.

A sterner teacher might have told her to start over until she came up with a potion that cured her spots. Professor Cauley, however, only pulled a small bottle out of her skirt pocket and handed it to Helen.

"I always have an emergency supply," she said, with something that looked suspiciously like a wink.

Helen immediately pulled the stopper out of the bottle and swallowed its contents. At once, the breakout disappeared, leaving her usual creamy-smooth complexion behind. "Th-thank you, Professor Cauley," she said.

"It's nothing." Dismissing her, the professor turned toward me. "Callie?"

I did my best to swallow the sour taste of unease in my mouth. Yes, it seemed that I didn't have anything to worry about, that Professor Cauley would come to my rescue if necessary, but at the same time, I didn't much fancy breaking out in spots in front of all my classmates.

Still, I knew I didn't have any choice.

Before I could lose my nerve, I dipped a ladle into the bowl before me, scooping up a large measure of the shimmering potion. It tasted cool and slightly sweet on my tongue—the spearmint, I guessed.

Otherwise, I couldn't tell anything different about myself. I raised a hand to touch my cheek, and it felt smooth as usual.

"Did...did it work?" I asked, knowing how foolish I sounded.

Professor Cauley smiled slightly. "It didn't do anything, Callie, because your skin was already clear. However, if you'd put the potion together incorrectly, it would have caused you to break out, as your friend Helen just discovered."

I allowed myself a small breath of relief. "I see."

Apparently, she didn't see the need to offer any praise, because after that the professor moved on to Juno and then Celeste, both of whom had also created effective potions, since their skin remained similarly clear.

Then Professor Cauley paused by Mona's workstation. "Your potion, Mona."

Mona's jaw was set, and for just the briefest instant, I wondered if she was going to openly defy the professor and refuse to drink the potion at all. Like her friend Philippa, she could have used it; while she wasn't exactly broken out in spots, her skin still appeared somewhat blotchy.

But then she picked up her ladle and drank from it. Everyone was watching her closely, waiting to see whether her skin erupted or smoothed itself to perfection.

Only...neither of those things happened. Her skin remained looking exactly the same.

Professor Cauley frowned, then stepped forward, producing her own ladle from midair. She dipped it into the bowl that contained Mona's potion and took a small sip.

No change that I could note—the professor's skin continued to look rosy and smooth, with absolutely no blemishes at all. Perhaps she had her own magic to ensure she wouldn't break out in spots the way Helen had.

Frowning slightly, Professor Cauley said, "This isn't a potion."

Mona stiffened. "Yes, it is," she objected. "I put all the ingredients in and stirred it exactly so. It's just as much a potion as anyone else's."

"I'm afraid not," the professor replied. Her voice remained mild, but I could tell from the way her mouth tightened that she wasn't very pleased with Mona's tone. "If it were truly a potion, then either one of two things should have happened. If prepared correctly, it would have cleared up your skin or improved it in some way. If it wasn't prepared properly, it should have made you break out further. Since neither of those things happened, I am forced to conclude that the liquid in that bowl has no more magic to it than this ladle I'm holding."

For just a moment, Mona's lips parted, as if she intended to argue the point further. However, she seemed to get a better look at the set of the professor's mouth and decided it was probably better to remain silent.

A nod—not in approval, but in acknowledgment. Professor Cauley turned away from Mona to address the class in general. "Occasionally," she said, "we have an outcome such as this. It is what happens when no magic at all has been brought to bear while a potion is being mixed. In these cases, the components of a potion cannot combine to become the elixir the witch is seeking to make because there is absolutely no magic involved in the equation."

Once again, Juno's hand went up. Mona's eyes narrowed; if she'd had any magic to deploy right then, I had no doubt she would have used it to blast my friend's hand right off her wrist. As it was, Professor Cauley said, "Yes, Juno?"

"Are you saying there's no magic involved because the person creating the potion doesn't have any, or because it just isn't manifesting itself, for whatever reason?"

I'm sure I wasn't the only person who noticed how carefully Juno had phrased the question. She hadn't come right out and said that Mona herself didn't have any magic, only whether that was something which could be a factor in situations such as this one.

The professor must have noted the phrasing as well, because she paused for a moment before she replied.

"It could be either of those two things," she said at last, clearly reluctant to make a definitive statement on the situation. "Most likely, it's simply because the magic didn't manifest itself this time. If someone doesn't have full control of her magic, there are occasions—rare, but not unheard of—when it stays dormant rather than working to make a spell...or a potion...effective. In this particular instance, it's not really a question of Mona not having any magic. She would never have advanced to her second year if that were the case."

Red flared in Mona's cheeks, and I almost felt sorry for her in that moment. It couldn't have been easy to remain silent and listen to herself being discussed as if she wasn't even present in the room.

As if realizing the current discussion wasn't exactly conducive to the preservation of a fragile student ego, Professor Cauley went on quickly,

"These things happen, Mona. I'm sure you'll do better next time."

Mona's cheeks went even redder, and she said in a sullen undertone, "I know I shall."

After that, the professor went on to have the remaining students test their potions. They all seemed to work well enough, and at the end of the class, she dismissed us to go to lunch.

My little group had barely sat down before Juno said, "Did you see Mona's face? She looked like a beet!"

"I rather felt sorry for her," Helen responded before biting into a pickle.

Since I'd had a similar reaction, I nodded. "Yes, that was a bit uncomfortable."

Juno gave a toss of her exuberant curls. "Please. She deserves it. It's hard to feel sorry for someone who doesn't give a darn for anyone else."

Well, she had a point there. Even so, I didn't think it was a good idea to pile on too much, if only because our roles could be reversed soon enough, and one of us would be on the receiving end of some not-very-comfortable criticism.

"I do not feel sorry for Mona McGee," Celeste said calmly. But even as Juno's face shone with vindication, Celeste went on, "At the same time, that was rather an uncomfortable moment. I would not have wanted to be in her position."

"I think it was great seeing the teacher's pet being put down," Juno returned.

We all knew Juno was referring to Professor Hendricks as the "professor" in her comment, not Professor Cauley. So far, Mona appeared to be barely scraping by in Potions and Kitchen Magic, whereas she and her team were once again winning the lion's share of the end-of-month trials in Intermediate Spells. There didn't seem to be a single task Professor Hendricks set before her that Mona couldn't beat.

While I had to privately admit it was good to know Mona McGee wasn't infallible, I also didn't think it terribly wise to crow over someone else's failures. "Okay…it was a bit fun," I admitted, and Juno grinned.

"Now all we have to do is hope she'll mess up like that in Intermediate Spells," she said. "Then maybe another team will finally get a chance to win a few points."

Helen snickered, and Celeste inclined her head, as if considering the prospect, and the conversation moved on to other topics. The whole time, though, I found myself considering Professor Cauley's words. She'd said it was impossible for Mona not to have any magic, because otherwise, she would never have been able to complete all those trials in the Beginning Spells class and have enough points to advance to a second year at the academy. That all made logical sense, and yet I couldn't quite let the idea go.

Had Mona managed to make it this far in school without any magic? And, if she'd somehow achieved that improbable feat, how in the world had she done it? I'd been keeping a careful eye on her all year, and so far I hadn't seen a single thing to make me think anything strange was going on.

Which didn't mean much. It wasn't as though I could watch her every second of every day. Besides, while I certainly would be the last person to heap praise on Miss McGee, even I had to admit she was clever. Perhaps there was some angle to all this that I hadn't yet been able to decipher.

Or I could be barking up trees for no real reason. Even Professor Cauley had stated that sometimes people's magic failed—especially people like us students, who still didn't have a perfect grasp on our powers despite spending almost a year and a half at Miss Primm's academy.

Holding back a sigh, I reached for my sandwich. It seemed that the more questions I answered, the more grew in their place.

Perhaps I would never get to the bottom of the mystery.

As we'd all expected, the day of the picnic celebrating the first day of spring dawned bright and sunny, with only a cloud or two here and there dotting the clear blue expanse overhead. Again, it could have been simple luck...or Master Marco's magic at work quietly in the background, ensuring that we would all have a lovely afternoon.

Because I wanted to have as much alone time with Lochlan as possible, I took him by the arm almost as soon as I got out of the car that had brought me and my group of friends to Master Marco's school. "Let's load up a basket and go exploring," I said. "There is still so much of the grounds I want to see."

Lochlan looked at me, askance, but he didn't argue. Perhaps he was worried that I planned to take him to task once again for concealing the truth about his family from me, even though I'd been careful not to mention anything about it in any of my recent letters to him. From time to time, a bit of irritation had floated up in my mind about the whole thing, although I knew he'd been silent on the matter simply because he hadn't wanted me to look at him as anything other than Lochlan Abernathy, a regular person who was fighting to manage his magic, just as I was. I had already decided I couldn't be too angry with him about that, since I didn't know whether I wouldn't have done the same thing in a similar situation.

"Of course," he said in response to my request. "We haven't wandered very far upstream yet—let's go there and take a poke around."

"Perfect," I replied.

We went into the pavilion where all the picnic supplies were laid out and placed enough delectable items in a basket to ensure we would have quite the feast. I noticed Juno doing the same thing with Dev, although Celeste and Isaac and Helen and Billy appeared be planning an outing that included all four of them. Because we four girls had already had a confab about what we intended to do at the picnic, neither Juno nor I had to worry that Celeste and Helen might be upset that we'd decided to strike out on our own.

Soon enough, Lochlan and I had left everyone

else behind. As promised, he took me along the banks of the stream that fed the waterfall I'd seen on the first night we'd kissed, now almost a year and a half earlier. The going was a bit muddy, but I'd worn sturdy shoes and hiked along doggedly, hoping he knew where he was going.

Those hopes were borne out within a quarter-hour, because he paused in a lovely open spot near a small rapids, where the fast-moving water chattered its way over the stones—and where either nature itself or someone from the school had set out a group of low, flat boulders just perfect for stopping to take a rest. They'd been warmed by the sun enough that they were very comfortable to sit on, and not damp at all. Lilies of the valley bloomed in the moist earth, and daffodils lifted their bright heads to the springtime sun.

I breathed in the sweetly scented air.

Perfect.

"So," Lochlan said after we'd spread out our feast and poured ourselves some water from the canteen he'd brought along, "is there something in particular you wanted to talk to me about? I assume it must be something serious, or you wouldn't have been so insistent about the two of us being alone together."

"I could have just wanted to kiss you," I returned with a grin.

His blue eyes glinted in the sunlight. "I

suppose so," he said as he returned my smile. "But I still have the impression that it must be something a little more important than that."

As much as I wanted to tell him that I thought kissing was *very* important, I knew doing so would have been a bit disingenuous. I wanted to be with him because his very presence reassured me, but I didn't know whether I was quite bold enough to say such a thing. True, we'd been seeing one another for more than a year by that point, but our discussions regarding the future had been purposely vague. How in the world could we make any real plans when we didn't know what was going to happen to either of us?

"It's been months since we were able to be alone together," I told him. "That's all."

He handed me a Cornish pasty and a bottle of ginger beer. "Is it?"

Did I dare tell him that I thought something very odd was going on with Mona McGee? After all, I didn't want him to think I was paranoid, or simply jealous of her success.

Then again, if I couldn't confide in Lochlan, who could I talk to? My friends, of course, but with something like this, I thought it might be helpful to have input from a neutral outside party.

Stumbling a bit over myself, I did my best to explain what had happened that one day in Potions and Kitchen Magic, when Mona's potion hadn't seemed to possess the slightest speck of magic…and I also described how I'd seen that strange silvery object she'd slipped into the pocket of her cardigan after taking her final exam in Beginning Spells.

Throughout this entire recitation, Lochlan wore a frown that gradually deepened. When I was done, he said, "All that does sound strange. But do you have any other evidence than those two instances?"

"Not really," I said, my reply delayed a bit, since I'd just taken a bite of my pasty. I swallowed, then added, "It's more of a hunch than anything else, which I know isn't exactly the sort of thing that's going to help me bring a case against Mona."

Lochlan scratched the back of his neck, looking perplexed. "Why do you need to bring a case against her at all?" he asked reasonably.

"Well…." I let the word stretch out because I wasn't entirely sure of how to respond. "Shouldn't someone—Miss Primm in particular—know if she's cheating?"

He didn't respond right away, probably because he'd also helped himself to a bite of pasty and was occupied with chewing it. At length, though, he asked, "Do you know for sure that's what's happening? Honestly, how in the world could anyone even cheat at magic? It either is or it isn't."

Those words sounded reasonable enough, even though I couldn't quite hold back a flicker of annoyance. Then again, wasn't that why I'd wanted this conversation in the first place, so I could have Lochlan act as the voice of reason to counter suspicions which might have been sour grapes and nothing else?

"I don't know," I said. "And I realize I'm going on hunches and not much more. I suppose I was hoping that maybe you'd heard of something like this before, since you're from an entirely different part of the world than I am and are attending a different school."

He shook his head. "No, I've never heard of a single instance of someone being able to fool the professors at Master Marco's—or at Miss Primm's, for that matter. But I can ask around if you think that will help."

As much as Lochlan's offer sounded as though it might be helpful, I could only shake my head. "I don't want you to attract any unnecessary attention to yourself. I suppose I just wanted you to know what was going on…if only to tell me I'm not crazy."

At once, he set down his bottle of ginger beer and reached out to give my hand a comforting squeeze. "I know you're not crazy, Callie. But I also think you might be trying to see a pattern where there is none. After all, up until the time you went to Miss Primm's academy, you were the only person you knew who had trouble managing their magic. Now you're surrounded by other girls who have a similar problem…but that doesn't mean it's the exact same problem."

"So," I said slowly, doing my best to think through what he'd just told me, "you think that all I'm noticing is the way Mona's magic is misfiring, and it just seems like cheating because her issues are very different from mine?"

"Something like that," he responded. "Or maybe there is something else going on. I suppose I just don't want you to do anything rash."

Because he cared about me, and didn't want me to make myself look the fool over a mystery that could very well turn out to be nothing at all. A welcome warmth moved through me, one that reminded me how lucky I was to be sitting here with him, to have—against all odds—found someone who listened to me seriously and obviously cared.

It seemed to me then that I should move the conversation on to a topic that was perhaps a little less fraught. "You're right, of course," I said with a smile. "Have you heard from your family lately?"

That question made Lochlan grimace. "Not bloody likely. We don't exactly correspond. My father will send me a card on my birthday, that sort of thing, but only because it's his duty, and not because he actually wants to. It's quite a disgrace for the Earl of Dundee to have a son with barely any magic, you know."

I reached over and took his hand. Even though his tone had been light enough, I could still tell how much it pained him to know he was a disappointment to his father. But because I also sensed he didn't want me to offer any kind of false encouragement or words of sympathy, I acknowledged the misstep I'd made in mentioning his father at all and did my best to move on.

"His loss," I said briefly. "But surely you've heard from your mother?"

"She writes me even less than my father does," Lochlan said. "Too busy going to parties and being seen with all the right people. Sometimes I wonder how she managed to take a break from the social whirl to have two children, although I suppose she thought it was her duty to provide the earl with an heir and a spare."

Truly, it sounded as though his family wasn't a very functional one. I reflected then how lucky I was to have two parents who loved each other and their children…even if one of their daughters was perhaps not precisely what they'd been expecting. Still, not once had they ever expressed any disappointment in me, even though I surely must have been an embarrassment to my father, an agent of DOME.

"Then never mind all that," I said, and reached into our picnic basket and pulled out a lemon bar. "Here—cheer yourself up with sweets. It always works for me."

He grinned then, the sober expression he'd worn a moment earlier gone as if it had never been there at all. "Definitely a good plan," he replied as he allowed me to hand him the lemon bar. After taking a bite, he nodded. "Yes, it's all better now."

"Beast," I said, and he leaned over and kissed me on the cheek.

"I've been called worse things." He munched away for a moment, and so I peered into the picnic basket, looking for the companion to the lemon bar he was currently eating. After retrieving it, I broke off an end and popped it into my mouth, reveling in the sweet-tart flavor of the icing and the richness of the cake beneath.

We ate in companionable silence for a moment, happy just to be together with the sun shining down and the friendly babble of the stream in the background. I reflected then how nice it would be if every day could be like this, with no worries about exams or trials…or neglectful parents.

But then, I supposed such an idyll would get

dull after a while, even though I thought it might be nice to try for a bit.

Lochlan finished his lemon bar and reached into the basket. After fishing around for a moment, he drew out a piece of shortbread. "Want some?" he asked.

Since I'd just eaten the last bite of my lemon bar, I nodded. "Absolutely."

He handed me some shortbread, then said, "Even though this thing with Mona probably has a perfectly logical explanation, I can ask Dev if you like."

"No, don't worry about it," I responded hastily. Although I knew Lochlan's offer had been well-intentioned, and I had no reason to suspect anything of Dev, I also thought it was probably a good idea to keep the matter just between us for now. The last thing I wanted was for rumors to start spreading through Master Marco's school and possibly make their way to Stanley Dolamore, the boy Mona had been dating. "I'm sure you're right, and it'll turn out to be nothing at all."

"But if it is?" Lochlan asked, concern clear in his bright blue eyes.

There was a very good question. I didn't know precisely what we would even do with the information I'd begun to gather about Mona McGee, although I thought if I came up with anything concrete, then clearly, I'd need to go to Miss

Primm with my findings. Although Penelope Primm was not exactly what one could call a hands-on headmistress, she at least seemed as though she would be concerned about any wrongdoing on the part of one of her students.

"I guess I'll decide then," I said vaguely.

Lochlan didn't appear entirely happy with my reply, but neither did he try to argue with me. Instead, he picked up his bottle of ginger beer and said, "That sounds prudent, I suppose."

After he delivered that properly neutral comment, we finished the remainder of the food in the basket, then folded up our napkins and laid them on top of any wrappers we'd left behind. Lochlan picked up the basket—much lighter now —and we began to make our way back toward the school. Neither of us spoke, but his free hand stole into mine as we walked, and a happy little flush went through me.

He wasn't angry. He'd understood that I needed to talk about my concerns, and would stand by and wait to see what I wanted to do next.

No matter what else happened, I knew that Lochlan Abernathy would always be there for me.

Another month, another trial. Sometimes Professor Hendricks gave us advance warning as to what we might expect from our monthly challenge, while at other times, she kept that month's trial a secret because she wanted us to practice thinking on our feet.

April's trial was one of the secret ones, and that was why everyone was looking at everyone else with trepidation as we all took our seats. I'd already resigned myself to Mona and her team winning yet another of these challenges, and so I tried my best not to experience a rush of nerves when Professor Hendricks entered the classroom.

As usual, I failed miserably.

"Good morning, everyone," said the professor.

Was that a faint smile touching her lips?

Possibly. The expression was so foreign to her

that I wondered what on earth could have prompted it. True, the day was a fine one, warm and with a fresh breeze blowing—the sort of day that made me wish I could be outside doing pretty much anything that didn't require me to be trapped inside a classroom—but we'd had plenty of fine days before, and I'd never noticed the professor appearing so cheerful.

Or perhaps she had devised a particularly tortuous trial for this particular month, and was looking forward to watching us try to master it.

"We've been focusing on interdisciplinary magic this year," she said, still wearing that unnatural smile. "And that is why your trial for this month will be to take what you've learned and put it in practice. Your task this time will be to write your own spell and demonstrate it for the class."

Right on cue, Juno's hand shot into the air.

"Yes, Miss Hightower?" the professor inquired, her tone dry in the extreme.

As usual, Juno didn't even blink. "What kind of spell are we supposed to write?"

"Whatever you like," Professor Hendricks replied. "Part of what you're learning during your time here at Miss Primm's is how to discover your own unique strengths and talents. You can discuss with your team what form you want your spell to take. Because you will be developing your own spells, we are going to take the entire class time for the trial. Be ready to perform the spell one hour from now."

Having given that pronouncement, she went and sat down at her desk. At once, everyone in their teams began talking, trying to determine the best spell that would showcase their talents without allowing too much opportunity for things to go wrong…as they so often did.

"This seems awfully risky," Helen said, both her tone and her expression dubious. "I mean, there are all sorts of ways a new spell can blow up in your face. I don't know why Professor Hendricks is asking us to do this. It seems like a recipe for disaster."

"Because she needs to find out whether we're capable of creating a new spell and deploying it successfully," Juno replied. Unlike Helen, she looked eager, ready to figure out the best spell that would show what she—and our team—could do. "Magic is about more than just doing what people before you have done for hundreds of years. Sooner or later, you need to spread your wings."

Helen didn't appear terribly convinced by this argument. "But maybe we should be spreading our wings *after* our second year is over. This still seems awfully advanced to me."

"No, Juno is right," Celeste put in. Although she didn't seem worried by the challenge the professor had given us, she also didn't look quite as eager as she might have been. "However, that doesn't mean we can't be cautious as we go about this."

"Definitely," I agreed, my display of caution earning me an eye roll from Juno. Clearly, she expected me to go charging into the task the same way she would have. "Let's come up with something that uses what we've learned from our various classes, but at the same time isn't going to put anyone at too much risk."

"Where's the fun in that?" Juno demanded.

"The 'fun' is in surviving to get to our third year," Helen said, even as she shot me a grateful look. It seemed she hadn't been entirely sure how I was going to respond to this challenge, either... probably because I wasn't known for my over-abundance of caution.

Since no one could really argue with Helen's comment, we put our worries aside and began strategizing. It seemed obvious enough to all of us on our team that Professor Hendricks was expecting a spell which put to use skills we'd acquired from across the curriculum, and not just in her particular class. Because of that, we decided soon enough that the best thing to do was create a spell with a potion component, demonstrating what we'd learned in Professor Cauley's classroom as well.

"And we can use your familiars, Callie, to gather the ingredients," Juno suggested.

This also seemed like a good idea. Flotsam and Jetsam had already proved themselves up to that sort of task on more than one occasion, and so I was sure they would do the same today. Or at least, I had reason to believe that even if our spell failed, it wouldn't be because of anything my familiars had done.

Potions, as we'd come to learn, often served a dual purpose. They could be something that stood on their own, like the skin-clearing potion Professor Cauley had tasked us with making some weeks back. At other times, they were only a means of focusing and directing magic as part of a larger spell, and that was what we'd decided to do during this particular trial.

In fact, what we'd decided to implement was a "lighter than air" spell. It required a potion that would be used to reduce the spell-maker's weight to the point where she could use her own magic to propel herself about the room.

"And what if you make it too strong, and the person taking the potion goes floating off to who knows where?" asked Helen, who'd obviously decided to be the voice of doom and gloom that particular day.

"We're not leaving the classroom," Celeste said

reasonably. "There's only so far any of us could go."

Helen pursed her lips, but appeared to accept this counterargument as a sensible one. At any rate, she raised no further objections.

"You'll need to take the potion, Callie," Juno said after Flo and Sam had returned with all the ingredients we needed for our elixir. "It just makes sense for the lightest of us to be the one who becomes lighter than air. Otherwise, the potion will have to do all sorts of extra work."

I wanted to protest, but I knew she was right. She and Celeste were both just as slender as I, but they were also taller, which meant they probably weighed more than I did. Helen was shorter than I was, a fact which didn't help her much, since she was also chubbier.

"Very well," I sighed. I didn't much like the idea of being the guinea pig, so to speak, but I couldn't really argue with her logic on this particular point.

Because Celeste was the best at making potions, she was the one who actually assembled the elixir, using a bowl she conjured from the Potions and Kitchen Magic classroom. As she stirred the mixture, I cast a wary eye toward the other groups. Louise Langford's team was busy scribbling something down on a piece of parchment paper, while Mona's team was huddled so closely together, I really couldn't see what they were up to.

Something that would fail in a spectacular fashion, I hoped, even though I didn't hold out much hope for that particular outcome.

"Fifteen minutes, girls," Professor Hendricks announced.

We all stared at Celeste.

"It will be ready," she said, utterly unperturbed. "You three all need to come up with the words of the spell."

Right. The potion was only one part of the enchantment we'd decided upon. We also needed to decide on the best way to focus the magic it needed through words.

Because that's really all a spell was—a collection of words and phrases put together to serve a specific purpose. It wasn't the words themselves that had the power, but the magic of the person reciting them.

In this case, me. However, I hadn't been using spells much lately, since I seemed to have better luck simply focusing my magic internally rather than using words someone else had written.

"I'm terrible at this sort of thing," Juno said. "Callie, you write the best compositions, so you should do it."

That was also true. The written part of a test was always the easiest for me. Even so, coming up with a cogent essay wasn't exactly the same thing as writing a spell, which was a lot more like composing a poem. Then again, perhaps I would have better luck with a spell of my own creation than I'd been in trying to utilize enchantments created before I was even born.

So I didn't argue, and instead picked up the pen from my desk and got out my composition book. Already, my brain was racing to come up with rhymes that would serve the purpose of the spell. Technically, a spell didn't have to rhyme, but some kind of rhyming scheme generally made it easier to memorize.

Inspiration struck, and I started writing quickly, quill scratching across the paper as Juno and Helen looked on in excitement. Celeste didn't have time to spare in watching me, since she'd finished brewing the potion and had to occupy herself with pouring it carefully into the bottle she'd also spirited away from Professor Cauley's classroom.

"Time," Professor Hendricks intoned.

A rustle went around the classroom once again, but no one asked for an additional five minutes. By that point, we all knew the professor was inflexible when it came to that sort of thing.

She looked over at my team. "What do you have to show me, girls?"

Celeste handed me the bottle of potion. The

glass was clear, and so I could see the mixture inside was an odd silvery shade and almost viscous in its consistency. Actually, it looked like molten silver—or perhaps liquid mercury—and I prayed that it was more edible than it appeared.

"We used an interdisciplinary approach to the spell," I said, sounding way too prim. Somewhere, someone in the classroom chuckled, although I didn't dare look to see who it was. Mona or one of her cronies, most likely. After pulling in a breath to brace myself, I continued. "Because of that, we used my connection with my familiars to collect the ingredients for a potion that will assist me in working the spell. Using those ingredients, Celeste made the potion that I will now drink."

My voice wavered a bit on those last few words. I really wasn't looking forward to swallowing the stuff. Yes, Celeste generally performed better in potions than I did, but she still had a couple of fairly spectacular failures under her belt.

Well, there was only one way to find out if this would be one more. If the potion turned me into a newt, I'd just have to hope that Professor Hendricks—or possibly Professor Cauley—could turn me back into a human being.

I lifted the flask and swallowed as much as I could in a single draught. To my surprise, the potion tasted quite pleasant, slightly fruity, with an overtone of vanilla. Just as I began to register the taste, I also started to experience an odd sensation, as if all my limbs didn't weigh what they used to.

Which was the point, of course. The potion reduced my weight, and the spell would allow me to move my newly weightless self about the room.

Since it seemed that Celeste had done her part, it was now up to me to finish the job. I pulled in a breath—but not too deep a one, for fear I might propel myself backward without realizing it—and then recited the words of the spell.

"*Body so light*
Capable of flight
Up in the air
Away from my chair!"

Almost at once, I floated up into the air. From everyone watching, there came a collective gasp, one followed by murmurs as I began to fly up near the ceiling, performing an entire circuit of the room as my classmates looked on, open-mouthed. Even Professor Hendricks appeared impressed; her brows lifted, and she made a series of quick notes in the ledger in front of her, the one she used to track our progress.

I completed my turn around the room by doing a quick midair flip before I landed back where I'd started, putting out my arms like a gymnast who'd just stuck a particularly difficult landing. Under my breath, I murmured, "*It is done,"* the traditional words a magic-worker would use to tie off a spell and render it inactive.

Only...I still felt oddly weightless. In fact, I had to grip the edge of my desk to keep myself from floating back up into the air. It seemed that I might have tied off the spell, but the potion was still doing its best to make sure I weighed nothing.

"Is there a problem, Miss Dobkins?" Professor Hendricks asked as she rose from behind her desk.

"No, not at all," I said hastily. Somehow, I managed to wedge myself into my seat, and then wrapped my ankles around the legs of my chair to keep myself firmly anchored in place.

She narrowed her eyes at me, but, to my relief, she didn't ask any further questions. As I sat, I felt myself getting gradually heavier and heavier, and so I knew the potion was beginning to wear off. Soon enough, I'd be completely back to normal.

Or at least, as normal as I would ever be.

"Miss McGee?" the professor said next. "Is your team ready?"

"Yes, professor," Mona said demurely. She appeared calm, ready for the challenge.

Well, of course she was. She'd already won all but one of the trials she'd been given this year, so why would she think this particular occasion was any different?

In my mind, it was. My team had done very

well, despite my lingering weightlessness. Mona wouldn't be able to walk away with a victory quite so easily this time.

"I'll be representing my team," she said as she rose from her chair.

Naturally. I wondered if the other girls in her group ever resented Mona's continual insistence on taking the lead during these trials. Probably not; if she'd failed over and over again, they might have had something different to say on the subject, but because they got to share the points she won, they were most likely quite happy to leave her in charge.

This time, she stepped away from her desk so she could stand near the front of the class. Professor Hendricks hadn't instructed her to do so, but I had a feeling that Mona wanted to position herself where she would be the center of attention. I had to give her that much—she was definitely one of the most self-assured people I'd ever met.

"Our spell isn't quite as interdisciplinary as the one Callie just cast," she said, shooting a sly look in my direction as I forced myself not to react. "However, I think you'll still find it entertaining."

After delivering that brief introduction, she took a deep breath and shut her eyes, obviously centering herself...or at least, doing her best to make it look as though that was what she was doing. Although she'd had her hands pressed together as she breathed in, once she opened her eyes, she put them in her cardigan pockets. Staring straight ahead, she spoke the words of her spell.

"Nothing by chance
Not quite a trance
Music enhance
Light now will dance!"

At once, the classroom erupted in light and noise. Colored beams of light crossed overhead, while a rhythmic thumping resolved itself into something that sounded vaguely like music, although it was no kind of music I'd ever heard before. And while it had at first sounded discordant, I had to admit that it possessed the sort of rhythm that made me want to get up and dance—or rather, I would have wanted to dance if I'd thought it safe to unwrap my feet from where they were holding me anchored to my desk. I wasn't quite back to my regular weight yet.

Mona murmured, *"It is done,"* and the light and noise faded.

"Excellent," Professor Hendricks said. She made a note in her ledger before adding, "You may sit down now."

Looking smug, Mona returned to her desk, while I did my best not to frown. I still thought my team's demonstration had been more spectacular—and probably useful—but it didn't matter what I thought. Only the professor's estimation would count.

After that, she called on Louise Langford's team. Louise announced she would perform a spell that would allow her to breathe underwater, an announcement which made Professor Hendricks' frown slightly.

"Are you certain?" she asked. "Some other type of spell might be wiser—"

"This is the one we came up with," Louise replied. "And we made a potion with ingredients brought here by Misty's familiar."

Well, then. And here I'd thought we were being so original by trying to utilize as many disciplines as possible to craft our spell.

After that, Louise nodded toward one of her teammates, who conjured a large aquarium filled with water sitting on her desk. That particular piece of magic seemed fairly impressive, and I found my heart sinking. Would my trick of flying around the classroom be enough to prevail against the other teams' efforts?

Louise then picked up the potion she and her teammates had concocted. It was a shimmering blue-green, like oceans in the tropics. After reciting her spell, she swallowed the potion and stuck her head inside the aquarium.

At first, everything seemed to be going well. A

moment later, however, she began to writhe and flail under the water, as if she were drowning.

"Pull your head out, Louise!" one of her teammates cried, tugging on her friend's arm.

Louise, however, seemed to be stuck. Three girls grabbed her as they attempted to pull her head out of the aquarium, but it appeared as though something was holding her under the water.

Professor Hendricks was at her side so quickly, I wasn't quite sure how she'd gotten there. She murmured something under her breath—a counter-spell, I assumed—and yanked a gasping and dripping Louise from the clutches of the cursed aquarium.

"Are you all right?" she asked.

"I th-think s-so," Louise stammered as she pushed her dripping hair out of her face. "I d-don't know w-what happened."

"Your spell backfired on you," the professor said. Now that Louise was clearly safe, she sounded and looked much less worried. "I think the third line was the problematic one. I would advise going to your room to change into a dry shirt. Come back when you're ready."

"Y-yes, Professor Hendricks," Louise replied. She shot a sheepish look at her teammates before hurrying off to the door to let herself out.

The professor turned toward the only group

who hadn't had their turn yet. "And finally, Eleanor's team."

After Louise's brush with death, none of them appeared terribly eager to perform their spell. An uncomfortable second or two ticked by, and then Eleanor said, "We're not sure if it's going to work—"

"You must try," Professor Hendricks cut in. "Remember that I'm here to intercede if necessary. Carry on."

They couldn't really dispute that assurance, not when they'd just seen the professor cut in and save Louise from drowning. Eleanor swallowed, then murmured the words of her spell without giving any kind of introduction as to what she would be attempting.

The only thing which seemed to happen was that the lights overhead glowed brighter and brighter, growing so bright that we all winced and lifted our hands to shield our eyes. Professor Hendricks appeared unmoved by this display, although, after a minute or so had passed, she said, "I think you can turn that down now."

Eleanor sent her a helpless look. "It wasn't supposed to do that," she replied, her own hand lifted to protect her eyes from the glare. "It was supposed to sparkle like the lights we have at our dances."

"Ah," the professor said. "I'll take care of that, then."

And once again, she murmured something under her breath, and the classroom fixtures returned to normal. I blinked, certain I was going to see the glowing after-image of those lights burned on my retinas for at least the next hour or so.

"Go ahead and sit down, Eleanor," Professor Hendricks said.

Looking dejected, Eleanor returned to her seat. Juno and I exchanged a glance. It seemed clear enough to me—and, judging by Juno's expression, to my friend as well—that there were only two clear contenders for the hundred points winning this trial would earn us. And frankly, I thought the spell my team had put together was the more impressive of the two, especially since Mona's team hadn't done much work to make their spell at all interdisciplinary.

But I knew my own judgment would have absolutely no bearing here. It all came down to what Professor Hendricks thought.

She went to her lectern and stood there for a moment, clearly pondering the conundrum. For just the briefest moment, her gaze met mine. Perhaps I was imagining things, but I thought I saw true conflict in her expression, as if she knew she should decide one way but wasn't sure if she could.

The silence in the classroom felt almost like a live thing, pounding against my eardrums. Everyone seemed to be holding their breath as they awaited the professor's verdict. I didn't quite know why the class felt so tense—this wasn't the final trial of the school year, and there would be plenty more chances for all of us to prove ourselves. Still, it was as if we all knew there was more to this contest than met the eye.

At last, Professor Hendricks said, "This one was very close. But in the end, I feel I must award the points to Miss McGee's team, since the lighter-than-air potion from Miss Dobkins' team didn't wear off when it was supposed to."

After delivering this pronouncement, the professor's gaze met mine again. This time, she looked almost apologetic, as if she knew deep down that we still should have won despite that minor bobble. What Mona had done, while showy, wasn't all that different from the magic she'd used to win other trials in the past.

Not that it mattered. Professor Hendricks had rendered her judgment, and once again, my team had lost.

Juno muttered under her breath, "What a rip," but luckily, her words weren't loud enough for anyone except me to hear them. I was inclined to agree with her—and so were a lot of my class-mates, if the startled and even downright angry expressions of those sitting nearby were any indication.

But we could have had the whole class on our side, and it still wouldn't have made any differ-ence. Once again, Mona and her team had won.

And I had no idea what to do about it.

CHAPTER 7
COVERT OPERATIONS

April turned to May, and May began to lead into June. It was hard to believe that once again we were coming up on summer...and the end of another year at Miss Primm's. All right, we still had several months to go, but we were still much nearer the end than we were to the beginning, and that was something to be cheerful about.

Or at least, it would have been if we had even the slightest ghost of a chance at padding our test scores with some points from Professor Hendricks' trials. True, Louise Langford and her team had won the contest at the end of April, thus breaking the winning streak Mona's team had been enjoying. Still, they were far ahead of the rest of us, and after miserably failing a test in Professor Cauley's class when the blanc mange I was making decided to animate itself and go running about the class-room until she fired off a counter-spell to render it to a pile of flabby, harmless goo, I could have used all the extra points I could get.

"But it doesn't matter if you fail a test or two as long as you have enough points to advance at the end of the year," Helen said at lunch one day in late May, where I'd been bemoaning that particular failure and absolutely certain I was going to suffer the same fate as Abigail Andrews and be shipped off to Mundania just as soon as the second year concluded. "And you're doing fine in your other classes. Didn't you just get an A on your History of Magic exam?"

"Yes," I replied morosely, refusing to be comforted. "But that was just a little quiz, not a big practicum like the test in Professor Cauley's class. It's certainly not enough to make up the difference."

Celeste poked at one of the cherry tomatoes in her salad, one eyebrow raised. "I am not sure it's time for you to be so doom and gloom. We have several months to go before we take this year's final exams. Also, I've been calculating all our scores, and so far, I don't think any of us is in too much danger."

Those words, so calmly spoken, should have

cheered me up. Celeste was not the sort of person to offer false hope, and if she thought our scores were all in the safe range, then they were. However, she couldn't see the future, and so she had no way of knowing whether a few more failures were lurking in our next round of tests. Too many of those, and I'd be sent off to Mundania to balance ledgers or shoot endless photos of toothpaste tubes or perform some other sort of mind-numbingly dull task.

Also, I knew I was probably cranky because it had been more than a month since our last outing with the boys from Master Marco's, and I found myself craving Lochlan's company. I wanted to hear his laugh and see the way the sun glinted in his coppery hair, and have him tell me that everything was going to be fine and I needed to stop worrying. I didn't quite know where he got his confidence, but I desperately needed a good dose of it right about then.

Juno stirred her spoon through her bowl of soup, leaving a kelp-y trail of noodles in its wake. "I'd just like to know how the heck Mona McGee can keep winning trial after trial the way she does. It's not even as though she's that good at magic—I mean, we've all seen her fail horribly in both Potions and Working With Familiars. If it weren't for her winning so many extra points in Professor

Hendricks' class, she'd be on the fast track to Mundania for sure."

Since I'd thought the same thing myself many times, I didn't really know what to say in response to my friend's comment. I gave a dejected shrug and took a bite of my turkey sandwich, belatedly realizing that eating turkey at lunch probably wasn't the best idea, since it tended to make me sleepy. However, it was too late to ask for anything else, so I thought I might as well keep going.

"I know," Helen said glumly. "It really isn't fair. It's like she has some secret that she's hiding from all of us."

Those words made me put down my sandwich and sit up a little straighter. Hadn't I been thinking the same thing for months, even though I hadn't come right out and admitted my suspicions to my friends?

"That's exactly it," I replied, relieved that someone else had finally put it out there in the open. Maybe now we could start to get to the bottom of all this.

"What is what?" Helen asked, looking startled.

"Mona *has* to have some kind of secret," I said, my brain working furiously, as though Helen's proclamation was like that odd Mundane stuff called petrol and had gotten my cerebellum running at high speed. "When you look at what's going on with her, nothing else seems to make any real sense. And have you all forgotten that odd little silvery thing I spied her slipping into her pocket last year?"

"Right," Juno chimed in. Her brown eyes had started to sparkle, and I could tell her thoughts were beginning to run down the same channels as mine. "She's *got* to be hiding something. No one could be as hopeless as she is in Working With Familiars and yet be able to beat every single challenge Professor Hendricks throws at her without having some kind of ace up her sleeve."

Celeste frowned. "It could simply be that her talents are confined to a narrow area of expertise, you know. That area benefits her because it happens to be the same field where we're able to earn extra points, but there doesn't necessarily have to be anything nefarious about the situation."

"That seems just a little *too* convenient," I told her. "And the time we had to write our own spells? I could swear that Professor Hendricks knew she should have given us the points for that challenge, but she awarded them to Mona's team anyway."

This particular argument didn't seem to impress Celeste; now she lifted a skeptical eyebrow. She wasn't the type to roll her eyes, but I could tell she refrained from doing so only by a supreme effort of will. "That sounds like...how do you put it? Sour grapes?"

All right—to the outside observer, no doubt my current suspicions would come across as nothing more than an excess of resentment at Mona's string of victories. However, I couldn't rid myself of the feeling that something much bigger was going on here, something that seemed calculated to ensure Mona McGee graduated no matter what.

"It's not sour grapes if it's the truth," Juno retorted, and I shot her a grateful look.

Helen's expression was a mixture of hopefulness and skepticism. "All right," she said. "Even if we assume that there's something nefarious going on, what are we supposed to do about it?"

"We have to gather evidence and then present it to Miss Primm," I said at once. I had that answer ready because I'd already pretty much come to that conclusion, even if I was a bit hazy as to what the actual timeline of such a process should be. "I don't think she's playing favorites, and she's not directly involved in what's happening in our classrooms, and so she seems like the perfect neutral third party to talk to."

"Besides," Juno added, "if we really do dig up some dirt on Mona McPhee, then Miss Primm is the one who'd have to do something about it anyway. She's the headmistress, after all."

Helen appeared satisfied by this explanation, although Celeste still seemed far from convinced.

"And what if you take this 'evidence' to her and it turns out to be nothing?" she inquired, one eyebrow still tilted slightly.

"Then we'll have made fools of ourselves," I said cheerfully. "It wouldn't be the first time, after all."

"But we're not going to make fools of ourselves," Juno put in. "Because we all know there's something fishy going on here, even if we can't quite figure out what it is. That's why we have to start gathering evidence, as Callie already said."

Celeste didn't appear very convinced by these arguments. "And how do you propose to do that?"

Luckily, I already had an answer to Celeste's question. "We have to break in to Mona's room and see if she's left anything incriminating lying around."

Even Juno looked a bit wide-eyed at that suggestion. "Seriously, Callie?"

"Seriously," I replied without batting an eyelash. "Where else would she keep that weird little silvery thing I saw—or anything else she might be using to make sure her teams wins practically all of Professor Hendricks' trials?"

"You saw Mona put it in her pocket," Celeste said. "It might not be in her room at all."

Well, that was a distinct possibility. However, I refused to allow myself to be dissuaded. "Maybe so. But I doubt she carries it around with her all the time, especially now that it's getting too warm to even wear a cardigan. Anyway, we don't know whether Mona uses the same device each time— whatever that thing was—to help her with her magic."

"If it's even a 'device' at all," Helen said. "I still think it could have been a good luck charm."

"All the more reason to find it," Juno said cheerfully. "Then we'll know one way or another for sure."

A little silence fell. Celeste still looked skeptical, but I saw the way she tilted her head as she considered our arguments. Deep down, she wanted to know what was going on just as much as the rest of us did.

"All right," she said at last. "I assume you have a plan?"

I did—or at least, the beginnings of a plan. It would require a bit of sacrifice, but it was one I was willing to make.

"Yes," I responded. "During Physical Activities today, I'll say I'm not feeling well and will leave early—"

"Won't Professor Crenshaw want to cast a healing spell on you?" Helen broke in.

"Not for a little tummy ache," I replied. "But it will be enough to give me an excuse to stay in my room during dinner. While everyone's downstairs eating, I'll sneak into Mona and Philippa's room and see what I can find."

"What if Mona comes upstairs before dinner is over?" Helen asked next, now looking worried.

It was a risk, but, I thought, a low one. Not once in the entire time I'd been at Miss Primm's—now going on twenty months—had I ever seen Mona miss a meal, or even leave dinner early. That was my main reason for going into her room at dinnertime, rather than trying to pretend an injury during Physical Activities or coming up with an excuse for leaving another class. I thought there would be too much risk of Mona coming back to her room unexpectedly in any of those scenarios, but during dinner? The odds were so low as to be basically nonexistent.

"It won't happen," I said firmly. "You know how Mona eats." Honestly, I didn't know how she wasn't as plump as Helen, since she often got second or even third helpings of her favorite dishes, but she somehow managed to remain quite slender.

Since Mona's appetite was pretty much an incontrovertible fact, no one bothered to argue with me. However, Celeste apparently felt the need to offer her own objections.

"You'll be in a lot of trouble if you get caught," she said. "Are you sure this is worth the risk?"

"If it turns out she's cheating, absolutely," I replied without hesitation. "Besides, it's actually very hard to get expelled from the academy. The only thing that's not allowed is cheating…so if I discover the truth, it's really Mona who's at risk, not me. The worst thing that could happen is that I'd be confined to my room for a few days."

My three friends traded uneasy glances. I could tell they weren't quite as blithe about the situation as I was. However, since none of them appeared ready to voice any more doubts, I thought the matter was settled.

Now I only had to put my plan in action.

* * *

On cue, during that day's Physical Activities class, I did my best to look queasy and wan, and about twenty minutes into our football match, I waved at Professor Crenshaw.

"Yes, Callie?" asked the professor.

"I'm not feeling very well," I said, trying to sound listless and not at all like my usual bubbly self. "I think that turkey sandwich I had for lunch is upsetting my stomach. Do I have permission to go to my room and lie down?"

"Of course," the P.A. professor responded at once…just as I'd known she would. "Do you need me to let Professor Cauley know so she might brew you a healing elixir?"

Since I'd been expecting Professor Crenshaw to make such an offer, I was able to reply quickly, "Oh, she doesn't need to go to that much effort. I'm sure I just need to lie down for a while. But if I don't feel better in the morning, I'll definitely see if she can help me."

The professor appeared a bit troubled at the way I'd refused a healing potion, but to my relief, she only said, "Then please—go on up to your room. I hope you feel better soon."

I essayed another limp smile, then gathered my things and went out. As much as I wanted to look over at Juno, I knew I didn't quite dare— there was too much risk of one of us cracking a smile, and I couldn't do a single thing that might rouse Mona's…or the professor's…suspicions.

Although I wanted to hurry off the field, I knew I needed to walk slowly.

Once I was inside, however, I had an entirely different plan in mind.

I hadn't breathed a word of any of this to my friends yet, but just a few days earlier, I'd discovered I was able to turn myself invisible. That discovery had been an entirely inadvertent one; I'd been in the loo and about to emerge from my stall when I heard Mona and Philippa's voices outside in the hallway. Since I generally did what I could to avoid them, the encounter seemed unfortunate at best.

"If only I were invisible," I'd muttered under my breath, and then...

...and then I was. I'd looked down and saw absolutely nothing at all, and neither did Mona and Philippa when they entered the loo a moment later. They'd brushed past me as if I weren't there, and I'd made my escape as soon as they were safely ensconced in a pair of bathroom stalls.

My invisibility hadn't lasted very long—I shimmered into existence only a few moments after I emerged into the hallway—but it was enough to prove I was capable of such a feat. And ever since that extraordinary episode, I'd tried to practice my strange new talent as much as I could, and was now at the point where all I had to do was think about turning invisible to have that particular bit of magic take effect.

Now I used my newfound gift to move swiftly up to my room, maintaining my invisibility until I was safely inside. Then I became visible again. So far, I still couldn't make the effect last longer than five minutes at the most, but it was still quite helpful.

I set down my books on the dresser and kicked off my shoes. Since it wasn't quite five o'clock, six-thirty felt a long ways off. Now that I'd committed to this course of action, however, there wasn't much I could do except wait.

I got out a paper I was writing on mistletoe and its various magical properties for Professor Cauley's class, and did my best to limp along. Some time after that, I could hear voices and footsteps in the corridor outside, and knew that classes had been let out. I didn't want to risk anyone catching a compromising glimpse of me when Juno opened the door, so I shoved my papers and pen under the bed and hurriedly slipped beneath the covers.

Not a moment too soon, for almost immediately afterward, my roommate arrived. She shut the door quickly behind her, but I was still glad I'd gotten in bed, because I could see a couple of Mona's cronies peering curiously inside during that brief moment.

"Still don't feel good?" Juno asked with a wink, and I shook my head. "I'll try to steal a couple of rolls from dinner and bring them up afterward," she went on. "I think anything else would be too messy."

"Some rolls would be perfect," I told her. "That'll be enough to tide me over."

She sat down on her own bed and said in a

lower voice, "Professor Crenshaw didn't seem to notice anything suspicious, so I think it's going to be fine."

"I know it will." I'd briefly considered casting some sort of spell that would allow Juno to send me a warning if Mona did end up leaving dinner early, for whatever reason, but had reluctantly set the idea aside as too dangerous. Neither of us had any real experience with spells like that, and I couldn't take the risk of mine backfiring in some kind of noisy fashion and alerting Mona—and everyone else in the immediate vicinity—that I was only pretending to be sick so I could snoop through her belongings.

After that, Juno made a few commonplace comments about the papers that would soon be due in Professor Cauley's class, and whether she should ask her parents to send her a new dress for the upcoming Midsummer Ball. I very much doubted anyone could hear us through the thick oak door of our room, but I appreciated her discretion all the same.

And soon after that, she let herself out, joining Celeste and Helen in the corridor so they could all go down to dinner together. Once the door was shut again, I sat up in bed and pushed back the covers. I could still hear voices in the hallway, and so I knew I needed to sit quietly and wait for at least five more minutes before it would be safe to leave my room.

Those five minutes felt excruciating, but eventually they passed. I got out of bed, and went over to the door and pressed my ear against it, listening intently. Since I couldn't hear anything except the thudding of my own heart, I thought the corridor must be empty.

Very slowly, I opened the door a crack and peered out. The only thing that met my searching gaze was a series of closed doors, with magically lit sconces glowing on the walls between them.

The coast appeared to be clear.

I opened the door a little wider and scanned up and down the hallway. It definitely appeared to be deserted.

"Time to go," I whispered.

At once, Flotsam and Jetsam emerged from their cage and climbed into my cardigan pockets. It seemed better to have them along, because their clever little paws would make my search of Mona McGee's room go that much quicker.

Hardly daring to breathe—and making sure I was safely cloaked in invisibility again—I exited my room and hurried off down the hallway toward the room Mona shared with Philippa. Once there, I put my hand on the knob and let out a silent prayer that it wouldn't be locked. Technically, our rooms didn't have door locks, but if Mona had decided to practice a locking spell, I'd be completely out of luck…unless I somehow managed to concoct an unlocking charm on the spot.

Since my odds of accomplishing that sort of feat seemed roughly on a par with growing a pair of wings and flying to the moon, I found myself infinitely relieved when the knob turned under my hand and the door opened a fraction of an inch.

I didn't exactly sigh with relief, but I did allow myself a quick breath as I entered the room and took a quick look around, shedding my invisibility at the same time. Like the chamber Helen and Celeste shared, this one was slightly larger than my own. Otherwise, it looked much the same, with its two narrow beds and a wardrobe in the corner, and a dresser pushed up against one wall.

However, it appeared that Mona and Philippa weren't as interested in domestic harmony as my friends—or as Juno and I, because the place was, frankly, an utter mess, with the beds unmade and books and papers scattered everywhere. Several pairs of shoes lay in the middle of the floor, so I had to carefully make my way around them. The last thing I wanted was to trip over them or kick them out of the way. True, the room was in such disorder that possibly Mona wouldn't even notice that her footwear had been moved out of its original position, but I still thought it better to be as cautious as possible.

I couldn't really tell which bed and nightstand combination was whose, and so I went to the one nearest me and opened the top drawer, even as Flotsam and Jetsam jumped out of my pockets and immediately scurried under the bed to poke around there.

The drawer I'd selected was filled with a jumble of hair ribbons and headbands, telling me it must be Philippa's. Mona never seemed to do much with her wiry black hair, but Philippa was very proud of her long, ash-blonde locks, and changed out her ribbons and headbands on what often seemed like an almost hourly basis.

Quietly, I shut the drawer and went around both beds to the room's other nightstand, while scurrying noises told me that Flo and Sam were still looking under the bed but hadn't found anything. Inside the second nightstand were bundles of letters tied up with appeared to be ribbons borrowed from Philippa. Love notes from Mona's sandy-haired beau, Stanley?

Perhaps. I wasn't here to poke into her private life, however, only to see if she was hiding something that had been helping her get ahead of everyone in our Intermediate Spells class. Still, I lifted up the bundles of notes, trying to see if she'd hidden something underneath them.

I didn't see anything, though. Disappointed, I shut the drawer and opened the one beneath it— and shut it again just as quickly, since it was filled with messy stacks of underthings.

Don't be squeamish, I scolded myself. *What better place to hide something you don't want anyone to find?*

Before I could lose my nerve, I opened the drawer again, then quickly rifled through its contents. I didn't take any particular care in what I was doing, mostly because the contents of the drawer were already such a mess that I didn't see how Mona could possibly discover someone else had been rooting around in there.

Unfortunately, I didn't find anything that didn't belong in an underwear drawer—no strange little silvery rectangles, no forbidden good luck charms or talismans or spell bags. Disgusted, I shut the drawer once again and straightened, glancing around the room. Both the wardrobe and the dresser seemed equally likely suspects, and so I headed over to the wardrobe, mainly because it was closer.

Inside hung multiple sets of school uniforms, as well as more personal items of clothing—the dresses Mona and Philippa had worn to the various dances that had been held during the past year and a half, jumpers and casual shirts and even a pretty embroidered skirt that I'd seen on Philippa during one of the summer picnics. On the floor of the wardrobe were several pairs of shoes. I picked each shoe up in order and shook it, hoping something might fall out, but I had no luck there, either.

As I glanced upward, however, I noticed a box covered in floral paper sitting on the wardrobe's one and only shelf. At once, I reached for the box and brought it down. It was around a foot square and about six inches deep, and rattled slightly as I brought it toward me.

That sounded much more promising.

I set the box down on the dresser and lifted the lid. Inside was an assortment of objects I didn't recognize, several of them metallic, most of them rectangular in shape.

What on earth?

No, actually…I *did* recognize one of them. It was the silvery rectangle I'd spied Mona slipping into her pocket all those months ago. One side was black, one silver. On the silver side, it had several buttons with tiny lettering underneath. One said "ON," one said "OFF," and the third button was marked "FLICKER."

As I stared down at the object, trying to decide what in the world it could be, the most frightening sound in the world interrupted my inspection.

The creak of a door opening.

I whirled, too startled to even attempt my invisibility spell. Mona stood in the doorway, hands on her hips, eyes narrowed.

"What on earth are you doing in my room?" she demanded.

CHAPTER 8
CRIME AND PUNISHMENT

This was definitely not the interview with Miss Primm I had been anticipating. I sat in one of the chairs in front of her desk, while Mona McGee occupied the other. The headmistress regarded both of us with puzzled dark eyes.

"Callie, you do know that you're not allowed to enter another student's room without her permission, don't you?" Miss Primm inquired. She seemed more disappointed in me than angry, which under other circumstances might have been some occasion for relief.

Unfortunately, I was feeling anything but relieved. How in the world had Mona even known someone had gone in her room? She should have been safely down in the dining hall, eating her fill of roast beef and Yorkshire pudding. The single good thing about my current situation was that at least Flo and Sam had managed to escape into the hallway, slipping unnoticed out the door while Mona had glared at me and demanded what I was doing.

"Yes, I know we're not supposed to do that without permission," I said. As soon as I'd been discovered, I'd vowed to myself to keep my invisibility charm a secret. Better that the headmistress had no idea precisely what I was capable of. "But I only went in Mona's room because I was driven to it."

Mona let out a short bark of a laugh at that statement. "Oh, I see," she said, voice dripping with derision. "Who held a wand to your head and forced you to go in there?"

"That's not what I meant," I replied, forcing myself to keep my gaze fixed on Miss Primm. Mona McGee was a lost cause, but perhaps—just perhaps—I could get the headmistress to see my side of things and realize I wasn't the guilty party here. "The only reason I was in her room at all was that I needed to find proof that she's been cheating all along."

Those words made Mona begin to splutter angrily, but Miss Primm only said, in a cool clear voice that overrode my fellow student's protests, "That's a very serious accusation to make, Callie. Why on earth would you think such a thing?"

"Because she wins far too many of Professor Hendricks' trials!" I responded without hesitation.

At once, Mona laughed again. "This is ridiculous. Of course Callie wants to believe I've been cheating—it's far easier than admitting what a terrible witch she is!"

Miss Primm raised a hand, her expression reproving. "That is enough, Mona. We are not here to cast aspersions on the individual skills of the girls attending this academy. Those skills will be measured by the exams given by the professors, and shouldn't be judged by anyone else. What I am trying to determine is why Callie would make such an accusation at all."

"It's because I know I'm telling the truth," I said. I made sure to keep my attention fixed on the headmistress, and not on the angry girl in the chair next to mine. "Ask Mona what's in that flower-covered box of hers—I'd really like to hear her explanation."

"What box?" Mona asked, her expression all innocence.

I scowled at her, even as foreboding began to creep over me. True, I'd watched her shove the box back in the wardrobe after she yanked it from my hands...but what if she'd somehow managed to make it disappear?

No, that didn't make much sense. If my suspicions were right—and I still had every reason to think they were—then Mona should have had no more luck getting a sturdy cardboard box to vanish into thin air than she would getting her rat Silas to follow her commands.

Voice steady, I said, "The box in your wardrobe. The one with all those strange gadgets in it."

"I don't know what you're talking about," she returned, still trying to look innocent...or at least, as innocent as those brows would allow her to appear.

"Well," Miss Primm said briskly, "I think it should be easy enough to clear this up. Mona, we'll all go to your room and look in the wardrobe."

"Of course," Mona said.

Her easy acquiescence only increased my misgivings, but there wasn't much I could do right then except go along and see what happened next.

"Excellent," said Miss Primm.

The headmistress got up from her chair, and so the two of us rose as well. I shot a sideways glance at Mona as I did my best to figure out exactly what she was up to. She'd been alone when she confronted me in her room, with Philippa nowhere in sight, and so it didn't seem as though she should have been able to spirit the box with its incriminating evidence away.

Then again, this was Mona McGee, slippery as

a snake. I knew I shouldn't trust her, even if I couldn't quite figure out how she might have managed to wriggle out of her current predicament.

Without looking to see whether we were following, Miss Primm swept out of her office and down the first-floor hallway, headed for the staircase that led to the second floor. At that hour of the evening, all the students were tucked away in their rooms, and so there was no one around to see us climb the steps and then make our way down the corridor to the room Mona shared with Philippa. It seemed she had some care for her roommate, because she knocked on the door first, saying, "Philippa? Is it all right to come inside? I have Miss Primm with me."

At once, a muffled but still startled-sounding, "Come in," sounded from inside the room.

Mona turned the knob, and we all entered. Philippa, who was sitting on her bed but obviously hadn't begun getting ready for sleep, looked even more shocked to see me come in, with Miss Primm a few feet behind.

However, Mona didn't seem as though she intended to bother with explanations, because she went straight for the wardrobe and threw it open. The top shelf was empty.

"You see?" she said. I got the impression she was trying not to sound too triumphant but had failed miserably. "There's no box. There's nothing in here except clothes and shoes."

Miss Primm made the effort to peer inside the wardrobe, but obviously, no box was in evidence.

I knotted my fingers in the hem of my skirt. "What did you do with it?" I demanded.

Mona widened her eyes at me. "I didn't do anything because there was no box to begin with. You're just trying to get me in trouble because you can't stand the fact that my team is doing so much better than yours."

Desperate, I stared up at Miss Primm, silently praying for her to believe me. "There was a box, Miss Primm, I swear it. It had all these strange devices in it—items that looked as though they were made to control something—they said 'off' and 'on'—but I don't know what they were for because I've never seen anything like them before."

Mona let out a disbelieving laugh. "You have quite the imagination, Callie. Too bad we don't have a class on fiction writing, because you certainly would get full points for that kind of story."

In contrast to Mona's mocking, Miss Primm appeared genuinely concerned. "You're sure that's what you saw?"

"Yes," I replied. "I know it sounds mad, but it's the truth."

For a long moment, she didn't reply. Then she said gently, "I want to believe you, Callie, but since the box isn't here, there's not much I can do."

Apparently, Mona didn't care for the head-mistress's comment, because she said, "Miss Primm, you need to punish her for breaking into my room—*and* for making up lies about me. She shouldn't be able to get away with that sort of behavior."

This time, there was something about the way Miss Primm hesitated that worried me. When she spoke, my spirits fell at once.

"I'm afraid Mona is right," she said. "Your rooms are supposed to be your sanctuaries, and it's simply not right to go into someone's private space and start poking around, no matter what might be motivating you." Another pause, and she went on, "Because of this infraction, I'm afraid I'll have to suspend your extracurricular activities for the next month. That means no picnic next week...and no Midsummer Ball, either."

I stared at Miss Primm, not wanting to believe those horrible words. Surely she wasn't going to hand down such a heavy punishment for what I could only view as a tiny little transgression. But her stern expression didn't change. For the first time, I realized that drawing the headmistress's attention wasn't necessarily a good thing.

Before I could speak, she added, "And now I think it's time for you to go to your room."

The sternness in her tone allowed no argument. I only said, "Yes, Miss Primm," and left Mona's room—but not before I caught a glimpse of the triumphant look she and Philippa exchanged.

Somehow, they'd managed to fool the headmistress...but they couldn't fool me.

* * *

"A WHOLE *MONTH*?" JUNO DEMANDED, sounding aghast.

I'd gone back to my room and gotten ready for bed. It wasn't until I'd turned off the light and slid under the covers that I felt able to tell my friend the whole sad story. Because it was dark, I couldn't see Juno's face, but I assumed her expression was appropriately outraged.

"Yes, a whole month," I said wearily. Sometime soon, I'd need to write Lochlan and let him know that he wouldn't be able to see me until early July, but that tragic task could wait until the following day. "Miss Primm didn't sound overly happy about doing it. I suppose I can take some comfort from that. However, it doesn't change the fact that I won't get to do anything fun for a *very* long time."

Juno shifted in her bed, sheets rustling in the darkness. "But you're sure you really saw something in that box."

"*Very* sure. I don't know what those devices were for or what they did, exactly, but they have to have something to do with the way Mona keeps winning these trials. In fact…." I paused there as a wild suspicion began to grow in my mind.

"In fact what?"

I pulled in a breath. Should I tell Juno what I was thinking, or should I hold back? Surely if I confessed to her the suspicion that had just started to roil my thoughts, she'd think I was mad.

But she was the best friend I'd ever had, and I didn't want to withhold any theories from her, no matter how crazy they might sound. Speaking quickly so I wouldn't have time to lose my nerve, I said, "In fact, they looked like something that might have come right out of Mundania."

Judging by the creaking that emanated from Juno's bed right then, I thought she must have sat bolt upright. "Say *what?*"

"They looked like something from Mundania," I replied, the notion more solid now that I'd said it aloud several times. "Or at least, what I think something from there *might* look like. Don't they have a lot of technology? Don't they use it to do the sort of things we can do with magic instead?"

"Ye-es," Juno replied, drawing out the syllable, her tone clearly reluctant. "But how could Mona even get gadgets from Mundania?"

I'd already come to the conclusion that there was only one plausible explanation for the source of those devices. "Her father works for DOME, doesn't he?"

Juno was silent for a moment. "Well, yes, but...." The words trailed off, and she fell quiet again. After an awkward moment passed, she said, "I thought it was illegal to import artifacts from Mundania."

"It is," I replied. "My father told all of us that same thing over and over again whenever we tried to get him to show us what it was like by bringing back a few harmless objects. But what if Mr. McGee has ignored that law and given his daughter the tools she needs to pass Intermediate Spells—and Beginning Spells last year, too?"

"That's quite an accusation," Juno said, then hurriedly added, "It's not that I don't believe you. It's just that I don't see how you'll be able to get anyone else to."

I'd already arrived at much the same conclusion. "I know," I replied, my voice sounding deflated even to me. "That was why I needed to have concrete evidence to show Miss Primm. But Mona spirited it away somehow."

A brief silence, and then Juno said, "That's the

part I can't figure out. You said Philippa wasn't even there when Mona discovered you snooping in her things. Otherwise, it would seem logical to assume Philippa was the one who hid the box after you were sent to talk to Miss Primm."

Honestly, I hadn't been able to figure it out, either. As soon as Mona had confronted me, she'd called out for help, and a crowd of girls had surrounded us, preventing me from trying to grab the floral box away from her. Professor Hendricks had arrived on the scene to see what the commotion was all about, and then had immediately marched me and Mona down to the headmistress's office. When we'd left, the box had still been sitting on the dresser where Mona had left it.

"Philippa *had* to have moved it," I said. "She wasn't there to see the ruckus—I think she was probably in the loo getting ready for bed—but she must have spotted the box when she came back to the room. It's entirely possible that Mona has let her in on the secret, and so she knew to hide the thing when she saw it sitting out."

"And now they know you're hip to their game, so who knows where it's been hidden," Juno said, sounding even more morose than I did.

I let out a sigh. "Exactly. I guess the real question now is whether Mona is going to be more discreet in her use of those devices, since she knows I know what she's up to...even if no one else will believe me."

"I doubt it," Juno said darkly. "If anything, she'll probably get bolder. She's exactly the type of person to rub that sort of thing in your face."

Since I had to agree with Juno's assessment, about the only thing I could do was shrug. Not that she could see me, as the room remained dark, but that was all I had energy for right then.

Apparently guessing at my mood, she went on, "But that's all right. I know what to look for now—and we'll make sure Helen and Celeste do as well. Sooner or later, Miss McGee is going to mess up, and we'll be there to catch her when she does."

I wanted to agree with that optimistic appraisal of the situation. However, Mona had been getting away with her duplicity for almost two years now. It was probably foolish to think she'd slip up badly enough that one of the professors would catch her in the act.

As far as her father's involvement went—if that was even the case, although I couldn't think of who else might be helping her—I didn't know what to do about that. If I were allowed to see my parents in person, then I'd probably be able to summon the courage to tell my father about my suspicions. But because I could only write, and because I had no idea whether all the letters that came and went from the school were being read by a third party, sending him a note outlining my concerns certainly didn't seem like a very smart thing to do.

"I suppose," I said, since I could tell Juno was waiting for some kind of a response.

"Don't let her get you down," she said fiercely. "This whole thing stinks, but she's bound to get over-confident and make a mistake sometime."

Perhaps, but Mona was so far ahead that it seemed her victory was already guaranteed. I knew some people would have said our time at Miss Primm's wasn't supposed to be a competition, but it was difficult to avoid that comparison when we had to go through those monthly trials in Intermediate Spells. The points earned weren't necessary to graduate, of course, and yet they certainly made matters much easier.

Fighting back another sigh, I replied, "I know. And I'm not going to give up. I just hate the thought of spending the next month with absolutely nothing to break up the monotony."

Juno made a sympathetic noise. "That was a crappy thing to do. If Miss Primm thought you needed some kind of punishment, keeping you from going to the picnic this weekend should have been enough. But making you miss the Midsummer Ball, too? That's beyond harsh."

I agreed. Unfortunately, I knew that the headmistress wasn't going to budge when it came to my punishment. Students rarely stepped out of line at the academy, but when they did, they needed to know there were very real consequences for their actions.

"There's no point in arguing about it, though," I said. "I could see that Miss Primm meant business. Honestly, the worst part is going to be telling Lochlan. He's going to be so disappointed."

And I wasn't saying that merely to puff myself up. Every occasion we were able to spend time together had become infinitely precious to us. We hadn't spoken much about the future—how could we, when it was so uncertain?—but we'd both come to the understanding that there wasn't anyone else we would rather be with. To have not one, but two chances to spend time together taken from us seemed beyond unfair.

Of course, by that point in my existence, I should have already realized that life wasn't fair. If it were, I should have been able to practice magic as gracefully and effortlessly as my parents or my siblings, rather than struggling with it as if it were some kind of wild horse that didn't want to be tamed to the bridle.

Lochlan and I would get through this. June would pass, and in July, there would be another picnic to break up the rounds of endless study as we all got ready for our second-year final examinations. We would have two weeks after that to spend together in August…assuming we both passed, of course.

But we would. No matter what else happened, I had to make sure of that. Mona could win every trial by cheating with her stolen Mundane devices, but she couldn't do anything to alter the scores I received on my tests in History of Magic, or Potions and Kitchen Magic—or even in Intermediate Spells.

And in the meantime, I would keep watching. As Juno had said, there would be plenty of opportunities to catch Mona in the act. No doubt she'd know we were scrutinizing her every movement, and so I assumed she'd be more careful moving forward, even if doing so might conflict with her desire to crow about her current victory. Even so, I had to believe the chance to show her for the fraud she was had to present itself at some point.

When it did, we would be ready.

As I'd thought, Lochlan was upset to learn of my house arrest, although, being Lochlan, he didn't accuse me of being foolhardy or careless, the way some people might have. No, he only said he was sorry that we wouldn't get to see each other, even as he told me I needed to be careful.

"I don't know much about this Mona," he wrote a few days after I'd sent him a letter with a carefully worded recital of what had happened to me. "But I know she's seeing Stanley Dolamore, and he's a nasty bit of work. Definitely not above cheating, even though none of us has been able to catch him at it. If she's fine with associating with someone like that, then it tells me she doesn't have many scruples. I would hate to think of something worse than being barred for social activities happening to you."

Since I didn't really want to think of such things, either, I did my best to behave myself in the days that followed. Sitting in my room while everyone else went off to enjoy a picnic on a bright, cheery day at the beginning of June was difficult, but I told myself there would be other picnics. Even when Mona did her best to crow about the lovely time she'd had—in a carrying voice that was clearly intended for my ears—I endeavored to ignore her and focus on my schoolwork. After all, that was the real reason I was attending the school in the first place. Mona could have her petty victories.

It seemed she was attempting to be circumspect, because her team didn't win the trial at the end of May. That victory went to Misty Cantu's team, who were able to conjure a llama right in the middle of the classroom and make it disappear again. I couldn't begrudge them their points, not when they'd succeeded so spectacularly.

But as we moved on into the middle of June and chatter got louder and louder about the upcoming Midsummer Ball, I found that the hard-won composure I'd tried to wear like a garment was beginning to get rather frayed. It was hard to listen to my friends and classmates talk about the new dresses they'd be wearing and how much they were looking forward to seeing the boys again. By that point, it had been more than six weeks since I'd last seen Lochlan, and I didn't know how I'd be able to hold on until the middle of July, when the next picnic was scheduled.

Then, one day in History of Magic, when Professor Simms was droning on and on about how Prince Cornelius of Malta had used an invisibility spell to cloak his army and thus sneak up on his enemies unawares, it came to me.

My invisibility spell. Wouldn't that be the perfect solution to my problem? I could make myself invisible and slip off to the Midsummer Ball in the car my friends were sharing, and then, once we were at Master Marco's school—which was where the event would be held—I could go and whisper in Lochlan's ear, and let him know I was there. We could go off into the woods or someplace else where no one would see us, and I'd release the invisibility spell for a few hours. Afterward, I'd put the spell back on and ride home, with no one the wiser.

It seemed like a very clever scheme...except for the part where I still hadn't been able to hold the effect for more than a few minutes at a time. I'd been able to work that kind of enchantment in a classroom setting on small objects, like a stone or even Flo and Sam, and have it last for quite a while, but for whatever reason, the invisibility I conjured always melted away after a few minutes had passed when I cast it on myself.

Perhaps all I needed was more practice.

That was why I begged off from a Saturday ramble with my friends and positioned myself in front of the mirror in the bedroom I shared with Juno. Bright sun streamed in through the window, and I wondered if I was being foolish for staying indoors on such a lovely day.

But no—having a chance to see Lochlan was far more important than a sunny stroll through a meadow. I knew I needed to get the spell perfect and make sure it lasted for at least half an hour or so, or I ran far too great a risk of being discovered.

Flo and Sam sat in their cage, watching me with bright, curious eyes. Luckily, Juno had taken Fred with her, or I might have had to worry about him squawking about me disappearing right under his nose…er, beak.

Since it was a warm day, I wore a plain T-shirt and some jeans. My reflection looked tired and wan, although I told myself that was only because I hadn't been outside much lately, thanks to my extended house arrest.

Focus. I thought of my reflection, and of how it would look when I gazed into that mirror and saw nothing beyond the furniture in the room around me. Because I'd done this part often enough, it came easily.

If only I were invisible.

The faintest of shimmers…and then I was gone.

Although I'd done this before, I rarely had the chance to practice in front of a mirror. I couldn't help letting out a small gasp, even as I reached with one hand to pinch my arm, just to make sure I was still really there. But I definitely felt the pinch—and heard the next gasp I made, since I'd pinched a little harder than I'd intended to.

Without thinking, I leaned closer to the mirror, as if by doing so I might have an easier time detecting my own presence. Proximity didn't change anything, however. I was definitely still there, even if I couldn't see myself…although the faintest mist from my breath touched the cool glass surface.

I would have to remember that telltale, and make sure I stayed away from windows and mirrors.

Now I just had to focus on staying invisible.

Remain this way until I say otherwise, I thought, then stared into the mirror again.

I'd been worried that I might have already begun to reappear, but it seemed I was still invisible. That was an encouraging sign, wasn't it? After all, if I couldn't make this last, there was absolutely no chance of my sneaking off to the Midsummer Ball.

At that exact moment, the door opened and Juno entered the room. Before I could move out of the way, she walked right into me.

"Oof!" I said, and she stared in the general direction where I was standing.

"Callie?" she said in disbelieving tones.

"Yes," I replied, and her eyes widened. "I've been practicing with invisibility. What do you think?"

Her brown eyes were still wide with shock. "Um…why? Although I have to admit that it's a pretty cool trick."

"I wanted to cast the spell on myself so I could sneak in the car and go to the Midsummer Ball with all of you," I explained.

Some people might have attempted to talk me out of such a crazy plan. Juno, on the other hand, only tilted her head to one side and gave an approving nod.

"That's a good idea," she said. "Or at least, it would be, if you were actually able to turn yourself visible again."

"I'm working on it," I replied. "I've actually been playing with this for a bit, and before now I always became visible again without having to put any effort into it. I'm not sure why it's sticking so hard this time, unless I made my intention for it to last just a little *too* strong."

She put a finger on her chin and stared

thoughtfully at me—or at least, at the spot where she thought I was standing. I actually was a few inches to the left of that particular location, but close enough.

"Do you want me to try?" she asked.

I contemplated her offer for a moment, then shook my head. A second later, I realized she couldn't see me, and so I said, "That probably isn't a very good idea. Professor Hendricks always warns us about trying to reverse other people's spells."

"And yet she does it all the time in class," Juno returned.

True. But.... "That's because she's the professor," I said. "She's much better at this than we are. It's different when she does it because she knows she's not taking any unnecessary risks."

My friend gave a reluctant nod. "And you may have to call her in to fix this if you can't get it figured out."

Perish the thought. I could just see myself trying to explain to Professor Hendricks why I'd decided to try becoming invisible. It probably wouldn't take her very long to figure out the real reason for this sudden interest in making myself disappear...and I could only imagine what sort of punishment I'd get heaped on me in addition to my current house arrest.

"No, I won't," I said. "We've got a while

before dinner—I'm sure I can get this sorted before then."

"Suit yourself," she replied, and kicked off her shoes so she could climb on her bed and pick up the book she'd left lying on the nightstand.

It felt strange to have her there, studiously pretending not to be looking in my direction. At the same time, I knew I couldn't allow the fact that I now had an audience to prevent me from figuring out a way to extricate myself from my current predicament.

Very well, then. I'd wished for my invisibility out loud, just as I had on every other occasion I'd done this, since all of my professors always said it was better for us students to do so while we were still trying to get some form of control over our magic. However, doing that hadn't helped me at all in this particular instance, and so now I thought I had better bring my focus inward. After all, my greatest successes in magic so far had been when I wasn't trying to follow the rules.

Besides, I thought as I took a few steps so I stood once again in front of the mirror, *you really don't want to be speaking the words of the spell out loud when you're invisible. That sort of defeats the purpose.*

I pulled in a breath and closed my eyes, visualizing myself as I stood there in my blue T-shirt and

faded jeans, feet bare due to the warmth of the day.
Long, pale hair falling over my shoulders—hair
that was somewhat messy from my exertions—and
lips a shimmery pink, thanks to the gloss Juno had
given me when she decided the color didn't suit
her very well and actually looked better on me.

All the little details that made up Callie
Dobkins. I focused on each and every one of
them, willing them into visibility. Then I opened
my eyes.

Yes, that was definitely me in the mirror. And
I'd done it without even using the spell at all, only
concentrating on returning myself to my normal
state.

"Wow," Juno said, and I half turned to see her
staring at me, brown eyes wide. "I didn't even hear
you recite the counter-spell."

"That's because I didn't," I told her. "I just sort
of…made it happen."

Her brows drew together, and she pushed a
springy, tawny-brown curl away from her face.
"That's not how magic is supposed to work."

"I know," I said. "But…it did."

Juno set down her book and swung her legs
over the edge of the bed. "Do it again."

"I'm not sure if I can."

In response, she crossed her arms and just sat
there, looking at me. Clearly, she intended to wait

until I proved to her that turning myself visible again hadn't been just a happy accident.

Very well. I'd actually been wondering myself whether I could manage such a feat more than once. And I needed to know—the only way my plan could possibly work was if I truly did have more control over this one type of magic than I'd thought.

I stood very still, thinking of how it had felt when I'd first turned invisible in the loo, of how astonished I'd been that simply wishing for such a thing to happen had apparently been enough to make it so. And I thought of how that single sharp desire had apparently allowed me to focus my magic to do what should have been impossible.

Just like that, I was invisible again.

Juno gasped. "You did it!"

"I suppose I did," I replied. I sounded startled —and no huge surprise. It was one thing to believe I might be able to turn myself invisible with no more effort than batting an eye, and quite another to realize I'd somehow managed to do it once again.

One more test, however.

I breathed in, and out, and told myself that when I inhaled again, I would become visible.

And so I did.

"That's incredible," Juno breathed. "How do you make it look so easy?"

"I'm not sure," I confessed. "I simply think of myself doing it…and it just happens."

She shook her head in disbelief. "Well, here's hoping Professor Hendricks has turning invisible as our final trial of the year."

That would be nice, but…. "I somehow doubt it's going to be that easy."

"Probably not," Juno replied, disappointment clear in her tone. However, she cheered up almost immediately as she added, "But still, it looks like sneaking in to the Midsummer Ball isn't going to be an issue for you."

No, it didn't. There was no way I could safely write to Lochlan and alert him that I'd be going after all; I'd have to surprise him and hope he wasn't so startled that he gave away my presence.

"Yes, I'm definitely going," I said. "I won't need a new dress, obviously."

"Too bad. But going in last year's dress is better than not going at all."

True enough. My mind was already racing as I began concocting the perfect plan for attending the dance.

Being able to turn invisible was opening up even more possibilities for me.

* * *

As it turned out, sneaking away took very little effort at all. I put on the lovely violet-blue gown Juno's parents had sent me the year before, took some care with my hair and makeup —even though no one would see me except Lochlan—and then let Juno and Helen and Celeste crowd around me as we headed out to the waiting vehicles. Safely shielded by my friends, I walked with them to the car, then got in first and squished myself into the farthest corner of the back seat, moving quickly so they could all pile in after me without too much of a pause. Once the car door had been closed behind us and the car started to move, I released a relieved breath.

"Well, that worked," I said.

"For now," Celeste remarked. She had been the most worried that someone would still be able to detect my presence, even though I'd turned myself invisible and visible again several times in front of her to prove I could manage the feat well enough. "What if someone bumps into you at the dance?"

"They won't," I replied. I'd stayed invisible just because it seemed safer, but alone with my friends in the car, I wasn't worried about anyone over-hearing a disembodied voice coming from seem-ingly nowhere. "I can move really fast if I have to. Besides, you know I'm not going to stay in the main hall—I'm going off to meet Lochlan in an entirely different part of the building."

"There is still much that can go wrong—" she began, but Juno cut in.

"Oh, stop worrying," she snapped. "It's going to be fine. Anyway, we're going to stick close to Callie until she's safely away. Absolutely no one is even going to know she's there."

And although I doubted anyone was going to check on my room at the academy, not with the entire school's population—including the professors—in attendance at the ball, I'd still piled pillows under my covers to make it look as if someone was sleeping there, and Helen had surprised all of us by casting an illusion to make it appear as though some long blonde hair was slipping out across the pillow.

It seemed I wasn't the only one who was getting better at managing her magic.

Despite all my inner reassurances that everything was going to be fine, my heart speeded up a bit as our car came to a stop. We'd already gone over this, planning to have Celeste exit first, followed by me and then Juno and Helen, but I still feared that when the time came, we wouldn't be able to execute the maneuver as quickly as we'd hoped, and someone might accidentally jostle me and realize there was more going on than met the eye.

I stuck as close to Celeste as I could without actually bumping into her, and Juno did the same behind me, and so one of the other girls from our school would have had to physically pull them apart to insert herself into the space I occupied. Because everyone was busy hurrying away, whether to meet the boys who were their dates or simply to go in search of refreshments, it turned out all my worries had been for naught.

We'd already decided it would be safest if Juno located Lochlan and sent him to the balcony that had turned out to be our favorite secluded spot, and so as soon as it looked safe, I slipped away from my friends and hurried down the empty corridor. Luckily, the silver shoes I wore with my dress had leather soles, and so I was quiet as a whisper. Even if someone had been around—and they weren't—they probably wouldn't have been able to note my passage.

Still, I found I breathed a little easier once I was out on the balcony. Although I hadn't seen a single soul anywhere near, I thought it was better to wait until Lochlan arrived before I dropped the invisibility enchantment. I'd practiced it over and over, until turning invisible, holding the enchantment for longer and longer periods of time, and becoming visible again had become almost as natural to me as breathing, and so I knew—or at least, I hoped—that I wouldn't have any problems tonight, despite the anxiety that knotted my stomach.

A few minutes after I'd taken refuge on the balcony, footsteps sounded on the stone floor of the room just beyond. I found myself holding my breath, even though no one else should have had any reason to come this way.

Well, no reason except to steal a few kisses, just as Lochlan and I had made a habit of doing whenever we were here. Still, I hoped it was a little early in the evening for that.

His voice was a hoarse whisper. "Callie?"

At once, I stepped into the center of the balcony and willed myself into visibility, just as he moved in my direction. The moon was only half full that night, and so not as bright as it could have been, but I still saw the way his eyes widened.

"You really did it," he said. "Juno told me what you had planned, but I wasn't sure—"

I went to him and took his hands in mine. "There was no way I was going to miss the Midsummer Ball," I told him. "We might not be able to dance, but at least we can see each other."

His grip tightened—not in a harsh way, but more as though he needed to reassure himself that I was really there. "I still can't quite believe it," he responded. "When did you get so good at turning invisible?"

"When I had a good reason to, I suppose," I replied. "It really is the oddest thing—it seemed as soon as I truly realized that all I needed to do was focus on what I wanted, rather than trying to recite a spell someone else invented centuries ago, then it came easily enough."

He shook his head. "That's amazing. Have you tried doing that with any other spells?"

"A few," I said. "Mostly conjuring cookies from the kitchen after hours."

That reply made him chuckle, as I'd hoped it would. He let go of my hands, but only so he could run distracted fingers through his hair. "It definitely sounds as though you've made quite a breakthrough."

I hadn't really thought of it that way, but he was right. While I'd practiced with a few innocuous spells, I hadn't been quite ready to branch out and attempt something truly difficult. If a particular enchantment backfired, then word would get out soon enough that I was practicing magic without the supervision of one of the professors, and who knows what might happen then? I certainly didn't want to spend the rest of my tenure at Miss Primm's academy being confined to my room...even if I had a way of getting around house arrest.

"I hope so," I said lightly. Because I didn't want to dwell on this new expansion of my powers, I asked, "What about you? How have you been this last month?"

"As well as I could be without seeing you," he said, and that funny little flush of warmth went through me again. I only experienced it when I was around Lochlan, and so I knew it had to be his own kind of magic...or at least, the sort of magic that sparked whenever we were together. "No great successes, but no real catastrophes, either. I think I can say I'm safely on track to make a wonderfully mediocre showing this year."

He sounded so rueful that I couldn't help chuckling, just a little. "Mediocre is fine," I told him. "It's enough to get you through to your next year, which is all that matters."

"True." He took my hands again, this time to pull me closer. In the next moment, his mouth was on mine, and we shared a kiss all the more passionate because it had been so long delayed. He didn't hold it for much more than a minute, though, and pulled away, saying, "I know this is a secluded spot, but I can't help thinking it would be better if we went somewhere else. Fancy a walk in the woods?"

"I'd love one," I said. We were alone now, but I remembered how Mona McGee and her boyfriend Stanley had walked in on Lochlan and me in this very room more than a year earlier. I certainly didn't want history to repeat itself. "Just let me turn invisible again."

Lochlan didn't argue, but waited while I gathered myself and invoked the magic that would render me undetectable to the naked eye. He let out a low whistle and shook his head.

"I suppose I'll get used to that at some point."

No further comment, though; he stepped away from the balcony and led me through the room beyond and out into the hallway. While I would have liked for him to take my hand, I could see why he avoided doing so—it would have looked quite odd for him to have one arm extended like that for no particular reason.

Good thing, too, because we passed a giggling first-year I'd seen in the hallways at Miss Primm's, even though I didn't know the girl's name. She was accompanied by a lanky boy with hair even redder than Lochlan's, and they both started guiltily as they saw him.

Ever unflappable, he just grinned at them and said, "Carry on," as he continued down the corridor, heading toward the door that opened onto the gardens beyond. I had to put a hand to my mouth to hold back a giggle, as I knew that indulging in disembodied laughter probably wasn't a very good idea.

To my relief, we entered the gardens without further mishap, although I knew they weren't

Lochlan's actual destination. Couples wandered along the paths of colored gravel, enjoying the warm summer night and the light of the half-moon that hung overhead. None of those people were close enough that we needed to worry about bumping into any of them, but still, we forged ahead, moving past the orderly roses of rosebushes and box hedges until we reached the wildland beyond.

The two of us didn't pause, however, and kept going until we got to the clearing with the fallen log where we'd once sat and talked about our futures.

"This should be safe," Lochlan said, and I allowed myself to shimmer into existence as he grinned. "Much better. Does it take any effort to stay invisible?"

"None at all," I replied. "Once I've invoked the magic, it just sort of stays until I decide to reverse it. I must say, it is rather handy."

"Extremely handy," he agreed. "And it's nice to know that we have plenty of time, although I plan to keep an eye on things."

He reached into the pocket of his silk waistcoat and brought out a gold pocket watch, its case studded with tiny diamond and ruby chips.

"That's lovely," I said.

He shrugged. "Family heirloom. My father gave it to me on my sixteenth birthday. I don't have much reason to use it, but I thought it might come in handy tonight."

That it would. The cars that had brought us to Master Marco's school would leave a little before one in the morning, and I needed to make sure I was back with time to spare so I could lurk some-place inconspicuous and wait for an opportunity to insinuate myself into my little group of friends. Otherwise, it would be a very long walk home.

Lochlan returned the watch to his waistcoat pocket, then extended a hand. The next few moments were spent in making up for lost time, but after we both came up for air, we went and sat down on a fallen log, still holding hands.

"So, tell me what's been happening with you," he said. "I can tell there's a great deal you didn't want to put in your letters."

"Was I that obvious?"

He flashed a grin at me. "Only because I like to flatter myself that I know you."

I pulled in a breath of soft night air. It was faintly scented with the woodsy aromas of moss and decaying leaves, and with deeper notes that I thought might have come from the earth itself. "I think Mona McGee is cheating her way through the academy by using Mundane technology."

That declaration sent Lochlan's eyebrows shooting upward. "I know you told me you thought she was cheating somehow, but why would you think she's using Mundane technology?"

I launched into an explanation of what I'd seen in the floral box Mona had hidden in her room, then finished by saying, "And since her father works for DOME, that gives him the perfect opportunity to bring back anything he thinks will help her pass her spell-work classes."

"That's a fairly serious accusation," Lochlan said.

"I know it is," I returned. "But I also know it's the only possible truth." When he didn't respond right away, I tightened my fingers on his and added, "You don't believe me."

To my relief, he didn't hesitate as he replied, "I didn't say that. But you're going to need a lot of evidence before anyone is going to believe someone would put their reputation on the line like that."

"Even if it's to save his daughter?"

This time, Lochlan hesitated. The moonlight was just bright enough for me to see the way his mouth tightened and his eyes narrowed slightly. At last he said, "All right—I can see why that might be motivation enough. However, just because Mona's father works for DOME doesn't have to mean he'd have access to the kinds of artifacts you described."

"He's an agent, same as my father," I said. "He

knows how to go back and forth between our worlds. It requires very strong magic—which might also be why he's doing this. He doesn't want to admit that his daughter has no magic at all."

Lochlan's head tilted slightly as he sent me a speculative glance. "Do you know that for a fact?"

I glanced away from him, staring at the moon-silvered beech trees at the edge of the clearing. Their leaves whispered in the night wind, but unfortunately, they had no secrets to give me.

"No," I said. "It's only a hunch. I think it makes sense, though. During our very first Beginning Spells class, Mona told Professor Hendricks that magic rarely worked for her, and that it seemed as if it just wasn't there most of the time. After that, she started being able to cast some spells, but what if they weren't spells at all, but things she made happen with Mundane technology?"

"It makes some sense," Lochlan agreed. "But that still doesn't sound like enough evidence to prove your point."

"It's not," I replied. "But then there's how she can't get her familiar to work with her at all, or how she's on the verge of failing Potions and Kitchen Magic. I think it's because she can't fake her way through that as easily with Mundane devices."

Once again, Lochlan went quiet. I could practically see the thoughts churning in his head as he pondered what I had just told him. Everything seemed clear enough to me, but what if he still thought the evidence I'd presented was far too flimsy for him to admit that Mona McGee was using forbidden technology to hide a lack of magical ability?

"I believe you," he said quietly. "Problem is, I don't know whether anyone else will."

That was much the same thing Celeste had told me. I hadn't wanted to accept such an uncomfortable truth, but with Lochlan only reinforcing it, disappointment formed a hard lump in my stomach.

"Then what am I supposed to do?"

He shifted on the log so he was pressed up against me, then dropped an arm around my shoulders and pulled me close. "Right now? Probably nothing at all. You're on thin enough ice as it is, and the most important thing is for you to move on to your third year and eventually graduate."

"So, I'm just supposed to sit back and let her cheat?" I asked, not bothering to keep the indignation out of my tone.

"As awful as it seems, yes," he said. Before I could protest, he went on, "I'm not saying you shouldn't still be keeping an eye on her and gathering what evidence you can, but you definitely don't want to risk getting expelled. If that happens, you're doomed."

Dramatic words, but he was right. Expulsion meant immediate exile to Mundania, and I couldn't risk that horrible fate, no matter how outraged I might be about the way Mona—and possibly her father—were gaming the system.

"All right," I said, the two words barely more than a sigh.

He leaned down and kissed the top of my head. The caress was a simple one, but the tenderness of it made me feel all happy and squirmy inside. I honestly didn't know what I had done to deserve someone as kind and brave and wonderful as Lochlan Abernathy, but I knew I would have to endeavor to make myself worthy of his presence in my life.

"Now, then," he said, his tone much brisker, "I want you to promise me that you won't do anything to get yourself in trouble again. I know it was for a noble cause, but I don't like this sneaking around. I can't help but worry about what would happen if you were caught."

"I won't get caught," I said boldly. "No one has any reason to believe I can turn invisible like this, and so it's not as if they know what to look for. I'll just slip in with Juno and Helen and Celeste when it's time to go, and then we'll all go back to the academy with no one the wiser."

"If you're sure," he said, although I could tell from his tone that he was still worried.

Well, I would just have to think of ways to distract him.

I leaned in for another kiss, and we embraced, doing our best to leave our troubles behind us.

CHAPTER 10
CONFIDENCES

June thirtieth, and the last trial of the year, since of course all of July and the first week of August would be taken up by studying everything we'd learned over the past eleven months. Although my little group had spent some time speculating on the subject, none of us knew for sure whether Mona would want to continue her winning streak, despite the risks of using Mundane technology, or whether she would decide to sit back and let someone else emerge the victor this time.

"Or maybe we'll just beat her fair and square," Juno said with a toss of her wild curls. We'd all congregated in Helen and Celeste's room to give each other moral support before we headed off to class. "After all, Callie hadn't really started flexing her magical muscles the last time we had our final challenge of the year. This go-'round might be an entirely different matter."

I tried to make a sound of demurral, but Helen nodded, looking eager. "I agree. No one really knows what you're capable of, Callie. You might surprise everyone."

Including myself, if I got over-ambitious and had a spell go even more wrong than it normally did. "It really depends on what Professor Hendricks asks us to do," I said. "If it's the sort of trial where she needs to see our work, so to speak, then I won't be able to help much. The way I've gotten my magic to work is to do pretty much everything that's the opposite of what they've instructed us to do."

Celeste nodded in agreement. Juno shot her an irritated glance and said, "But the whole point of being here is learning ways to have our magic work for us, even if those methods aren't exactly by the book. Professor Hendricks said as much our very first day of class. I don't think she can take points away from you just because of the way you're now working with magic, as long as you get the results she's asking for."

I wanted to believe this. I truly did. At the same time, though, I couldn't help thinking that the professor would still find some way to make sure I didn't score highly enough to win.

If I was even the team representative this time.

Everyone else in my little group seemed to be thinking that way, but so much depended on what the actual trial would be.

We trooped into the classroom. My classmates all looked as anxious as I felt, showing that it didn't matter how many times we did this—every challenge still felt like a momentous occasion. So much depended on earning those extra points. According to Celeste's calculations, no one on our team was too much at risk of failing and being shipped off to Mundania, but of course, we hadn't taken our final examinations yet, either.

I sat down and did my best to look unconcerned as Professor Hendricks entered the classroom. She smiled at us, apparently oblivious to the obvious strain in the air.

Or perhaps she was so used to it by this point, it no longer registered with her.

At any rate, her pleasant expression remained in place as she said, "Good morning, class, and welcome to the final trial of the year. We've covered a great deal in Intermediate Spells, and I want this to be your chance to shine. Because of that, I'm going to leave this month's task up to you and your teams. You can decide what it is you want to do—but decide quickly, as we will begin in fifteen minutes. Assemble your teams."

After making this pronouncement, she went and sat down behind her desk. Chatter filled the classroom as everyone began plotting and planning.

Juno was practically beside herself with glee. "This is so easy!" she exclaimed. "We can just have Callie turn herself invisible and back again, and we're sure to win!"

"Not so quickly," I said. "For one thing, I'm not even sure I want Professor Hendricks—or anyone else—to know I'm able to do that. It's come in pretty handy, after all."

That protest made Juno's expression fall. "Oh, come on," she replied. "It's a spectacular piece of magic. And no one's going to suspect you've been using it for anything nefarious."

"I am glad you're so trusting," Celeste put in. "But I think Callie is right. We need to come up with something else."

A troubled silence fell. "Callie's also gotten very good at summoning cakes and cookies," Helen ventured.

"Summoning isn't fancy enough," Juno said. "Remember how Louise Langford conjured that aquarium back in April?"

"The one she almost drowned herself in?" Helen replied. Clearly, that part of the incident had left an indelible impression on her.

Juno waved a hand. "That doesn't matter. What matters is that she conjured it at all. We need to do something Mona and her team can't possibly beat."

We all went quiet for a moment. Then it occurred to me.

"What if I make all of *you* invisible?" I asked.

Helen's eyes widened. "You can do that?" she returned, looking both hopeful…and skeptical.

"In theory," I said. "It's really not much different from turning myself invisible. But it allows me to work with a kind of magic I know well, and it'll look pretty spectacular if I can do it to all of you at the same time. Turning other people invisible is generally thought to be much harder than making oneself invisible, especially if you're doing it to more than one person."

Celeste nodded slowly. "That could work…if you are sure you can turn us back. I cannot speak for anyone else, but I know I would not like to spend the rest of my life invisible."

"That won't happen," I assured her. At least, I was fairly certain it wouldn't happen. Besides, even if my magic failed me at the worst possible time, I had to believe that Professor Hendricks would set everything to rights. Part of her task as a professor was to correct any failed spells, after all.

"Then that's it," Juno said. "And honestly, I wouldn't mind being invisible for a little while. It would be nice to get another crack at those gadgets Mona is hiding."

"Shh," I said. "We shouldn't be talking about that here."

"Right," Juno replied, looking contrite. It seemed she'd almost forgotten we were having this conversation in Professor Hendricks' classroom, and not back in Helen and Celeste's room. "Sorry."

I gave her an encouraging smile. "It's fine."

We had to end our convo there, because Professor Hendricks had gotten to her feet and then strode to the lectern at the front of the room. "Is everyone ready?"

All of us nodded, although I could sense the beginnings of nervous butterflies in my stomach. I'd told my friends that I would be able to turn them all invisible and back again, but what if my skills failed me? After all, I'd never tried this particular trick before.

But it was far too late to back out, and so I made myself sit there calmly as the professor said, "Excellent. Let us have Mona's team go first." She glanced over at my nemesis, who sat at her desk a few rows down and looked remarkably uncon-cerned about the situation. "Mona, who will be representing your team?"

"I will," she replied, surprising absolutely no one.

"Then please come to the front of the class."

Mona rose from her seat and took her usual

spot a few feet from the lectern. Although it was a warm day, and our cardigans certainly not necessary, she still wore hers.

Because she has to hide those Mundane gadgets in her pockets, I thought sourly. *It's too bad that Professor Hendricks has never once asked her why she insists on wearing a cardigan when it's shirtsleeve weather outside.*

But since I knew there was no point in calling her out, I made myself sit quietly in my chair. Next to me, Juno raised an eyebrow and gave a significant nod toward the cardigan in question, signaling that I wasn't the only one who knew exactly what was going on, even if the professor was too blind to see it.

"Today I am going to create a wall of sound," Mona said. "You might want to cover your ears."

Professor Hendricks raised an eyebrow, but she lifted her hands, preparing herself in case she needed to protect her ears. All around me, my classmates did the same—including Juno, Helen, and Celeste. I wanted to resolutely keep my hands folded in my lap, but decided it was foolish to possibly harm my hearing out of pure stubbornness.

And then Mona lifted her chin and recited,
"From the ground
Wall of sound
Make ears pound

While you resound!"

At once, a sonorous wave of noise emanated from her where she stood. I couldn't even say it was music. Not exactly, anyway. Perhaps one long chord of deep, dark strings, so low on the register that it felt as if it was shaking the very floor beneath my feet. It held for a minute, possibly a little less, and then slowly faded away.

Professor Hendricks blinked. "Very good, Mona. You may sit down now."

Mona returned to her seat, looking pleased with herself. I had to say that it was a rather effective demonstration…or at least, it would have been, if I hadn't known that she'd made the whole thing happen through the use of some sort of strange Mundane technology.

After that, Misty Cantu got up and did her best to conjure a miniature storm inside a glass dome. Unfortunately, the glass shattered when the first tiny lightning bolt hit it, and the next few minutes were spent with all of us ducking under our desks until Professor Hendricks was able to make the pint-sized thunderclouds dissipate, disappearing back to wherever they'd come from.

Louise Langford didn't fare much better, since she was trying to summon an entire picnic and only had a couple of forlorn sandwiches appear on her desk. The professor thanked her, and then turned toward me.

"Miss Dobkins?"

I stood. "My entire team will be participating in the trial."

A flicker of surprise came and went in her face, but Professor Hendricks appeared neutral enough as she said, "Very good. All of you can come to the front of the class, then."

The rest of my team rose from their seats as well, and we all took up our positions, ranged a little ways away from the professor's lectern. Juno gave me a small nod, and I stood quietly for a moment, reminding myself of what it felt like to turn myself invisible, and how it would be easy enough to make that magic act on my friends rather than myself.

As one, they all vanished into thin air.

The whole classroom erupted in one collective gasp. Even the professor got up from her chair, peering intently at the space that had, up until a moment earlier, been occupied by three of her pupils.

"You made them disappear?" she asked, her tone indicating she wasn't quite sure what I was up to.

"No, we're right here," came Juno's cheerful voice. "She just made us all invisible."

Murmurs swept through the classroom, and Professor Hendricks blinked again, as if she wasn't quite sure whether she wanted to believe the evidence of her own ears.

"*All* of you?" she asked.

"Yes," said Celeste. "But, as Juno said, we have not gone anywhere."

"I'm here, too," Helen piped in.

An unwilling smile stretched the professor's mouth. "That is quite…impressive," she said, then glanced over at me. "I assume you can turn them back?"

"Oh, yes," I replied, glad that I sounded more confident than I felt. I shut my eyes for a moment as I recalled what it felt like to reverse the enchantment and make the unseen visible again.

And then my three friends shimmered into existence. Well, that was what it looked like, anyway. Of course, they'd been standing there all along.

"Very good, Callie," Professor Hendricks said. "You may all go sit down now."

I nodded, and my team returned to their seats. As I settled myself on the hard chair, I saw out of the corner of my eye how Mona McGee was glaring at me, her mouth set in a hard line.

The shoe's on the other foot now, isn't it? I thought with some satisfaction. Clearly, she wasn't very happy about my little demonstration.

The professor went to her lectern and stood behind it. "Thank you for all your efforts, girls," she said. "This was a difficult choice, but…." She paused for a long moment, her gaze sweeping over all of us. "The points for the June challenge go to Miss Dobkins and her team."

Helen let out a little squeak of excitement before she managed to contain herself, and Juno shot me a look of triumph. Celeste, as usual, appeared utterly composed, but I knew she had to be happy as well. Those points might be the extra cushion we needed to advance to our third and final year at the academy.

If looks had been daggers, I would have been skewered multiple times by the venomous glares I received from Mona McGee's team. However, I ignored them as I gathered my books and got to my feet, ready to share some celebratory sweets with my friends.

Just as I was about to walk out the door, though, Professor Hendricks' voice stopped me. "Miss Dobkins, a word, please."

Panic flared, even as I tried to tell myself there could be a multitude of reasons why the professor would want to talk to me. It couldn't simply be that she'd put two and two together and realized that if I could turn all my friends invisible, I could certainly do the same to myself.

I walked over to the lectern and paused there, hoping I looked innocent and utterly inoffensive. "Yes, Professor Hendricks?"

She gazed at me for a moment, gray eyes stern. "That was quite an impressive display, Miss Dobkins. One thing, however—I didn't hear you recite the invisibility spell. I wasn't aware you'd mastered subvocal enchantments already."

"I haven't," I replied, glad that my voice sounded steady enough. "I've figured out a different way to get my magic to work."

A pair of gray-frosted eyebrows lifted slightly. "Oh, you have? And how did you manage that particular feat?"

I knew that shrugging would probably seem terribly off-hand, and yet my shoulders seemed to lift of their own accord. "I—I'm not entirely certain. It's as if I've learned how to use my inner focus to make the magic happen without having to use a specific spell."

She stared at me, disbelief clear in every line of her sharp features. "That is not how magic works."

I made a helpless gesture, hands lifted slightly. "It's how it works for me. How else could I make all my friends turn invisible at the same time?"

"Perhaps they were the ones casting the spell," she suggested, her tone continuing to indicate that she didn't believe me capable of such a feat.

"No," I said. "That's not what happened. If that were the case, you would have heard them casting the spell, since they can't really do subvocal enchantments yet, either." I wanted to add that it had been all me, but since such a comment would have sounded horribly boastful, I remained silent.

Professor Hendricks was quiet as well, as if she couldn't quite decide the best way to respond to my words. After a moment, however, she said, "Very well. It was an impressive display. Congratulations—you can go join your friends now."

Relieved, I fled the room, glad that she hadn't asked me more questions I couldn't quite answer.

Juno and Celeste and Helen were loitering outside, obviously waiting for me to appear. As I approached, Juno asked, "Well?"

"It's fine," I said, even though I couldn't quite get rid of the nagging worry that things were perhaps not as fine as I wished them to be. "Professor Hendricks wanted to ask me a couple of questions about my spell."

"She's not taking our points back, is she?" Helen asked, looking alarmed.

"No," I assured her. "Nothing like that. She was interested in how I'd done it, that's all."

Juno didn't appear as relieved by my comment as I'd thought she would be. "You didn't tell her the truth, did you?"

"Well, of course I did," I replied. "What else was I supposed to say? She was a bit surprised, I suppose, but it's like you said earlier. She wants us all to be successful, no matter how we use our magic."

"And even if we aren't, and are using Mundane technology, I suppose," Juno remarked.

"Professor Hendricks doesn't know that," Celeste said.

"Well, she should," Juno said. "It isn't like Callie didn't try to warn everyone."

The fact that I couldn't get Miss Primm to believe me still rankled. However, knowing my team had those extra points in their pocket helped to wash away some of the sting. The situation could have been worse, after all.

"Ancient history," I said cheerfully. "I say we get some of cook's sticky buns and go enjoy ourselves. We'll have to be running around in Physical Activities soon enough."

Everyone thought this was an excellent idea, and so we headed off to the kitchen to cajole some treats from Miss Greenbriar. As we went, though, I couldn't help wondering what the other shoe was, and when it would drop.

THE NEXT DAY, AS IT TURNED OUT. WE HAD just settled down in History of Magic class to begin our review of that year's coursework when Miss Primm herself appeared and murmured a few words to Professor Simms. The professor glanced over at me and said, "Callie? The head-mistress would like a few words with you."

My heart dropped to somewhere around my feet, but I made myself get up from my chair and go over to the spot where the headmistress waited with Professor Simms by her lectern. "Yes?" I said.

If she was upset with me, or about to dole out some sort of punishment, Miss Primm's clean, elegant features showed no sign of it. As usual, she appeared lovely and serene, with the kind of calm grace I hoped I might one day be able to achieve.

"Hello, Callie," she said. "I thought you might take a walk with me."

Since there wasn't any way I could possibly refuse, I stammered a "yes" and followed her out of the classroom, and then down the central hallway and into the rose garden. At that time of day, everyone was in class, and so the two of us had the grounds to ourselves. We walked a bit more, and then the headmistress paused under an arbor covered in a riot of climbing roses, red and pink and white.

"I suppose you're wondering why I wanted to speak with you," Miss Primm said.

"Well...yes."

She smiled. "It's nothing terrible, I assure you. Professor Hendricks came to me yesterday and told me how you'd won the June trial in her class.

She also spoke of the unusual way you used your magic."

"If I've done something wrong, I'm sorry—" I began, and Miss Primm raised a hand, stopping me.

"Not at all," she said. "In fact, I wanted to congratulate you on stepping outside the bounds of what's always been taught and figuring out something on your own. That's not always an easy task for the students here, even though some, like you, would greatly benefit from taking a less orthodox approach to their particular situations."

I stared at her, not quite sure how I was supposed to take that statement. "Then why aren't we taught to work with magic in nontraditional ways?"

My question elicited a smile, although I didn't think she was laughing at me. No, I guessed it was more an acknowledgment that it wasn't as easy to change things as I might like to believe.

"Because some of our students would balk at such a notion," she replied. "Also, many do respond better to a more traditional approach, and only failed in their previous magical studies because their teachers weren't expressing ideas and concepts to them in a manner they could under-stand. Coming here isn't a punishment, Callie—it's an opportunity to make magic work for your-self." She paused, then went on, "Part of the reason I've tried to open things up these past few years is that I sincerely hope by being exposed to new experiences—such as being able to associate with the boys from Master Marco's—is that an engaged mind is a mind more likely to succeed. I'm sure some parents weren't happy with me for giving their daughters social lives, but I've been seeing a better success rate since I made those changes."

"But not for everyone," I murmured, thinking of Abigail Andrews.

Miss Primm nodded, her expression solemn. "Unfortunately not. There are always those who can't make it through, for a variety of reasons. On the other hand, when I hear of someone like you, Callie, someone who's managed to engage with her magic in a new and exciting way, I know this school is on the right track. And I certainly didn't want you to think you were in trouble because you went at your magic in a way that was different to how you've been taught." The corners of her mouth quirked, and she added, "Or because you turned yourself invisible and went to the Midsummer Ball despite your house arrest."

I stared at her, aghast. "How did you know about that?"

A small twinkle showed in her eyes. For some reason, it made me think of how she'd looked at that first Midwinter Ball, and of how Master

Marco had stared at her. Despite her easy, almost confidential manner now, I still thought it probably best not to ask precisely what her relationship with the headmaster might be.

"It's my job to know these things," she replied. "Otherwise, I wouldn't be a very good guardian of you girls, would I? Yes, you're all legally adults, and so there are limits to what I can and can't do as headmistress of this school, but still, it's my responsibility to keep track of you and make sure you aren't in a position to do harm to yourselves or to others. It's a small charm, really, just something that alerts me when someone is moving about the grounds unseen." She stopped there, dark eyes amused. "Or did you think you were the first student to use an invisibility spell to get around the rules?"

Honestly, I had, but I wasn't sure I wanted to confess such a thing. Doing so would make me sound far too arrogant. Rather than address her question directly, I said, "And yet you weren't able to tell that Mona McGee was using Mundane technology to cheat her way through Intermediate Spells?"

At once, Miss Primm's expression sobered. "I suspected something—mostly because her file showed that she had a very hard time of it until she reached her senior year of secondary school. Suddenly, she began to do much better, although not sufficiently so to prevent her from coming here."

"So, you've been keeping an eye on her," I said. That revelation made me feel a bit better. No, Miss Primm hadn't been able to catch Mona in the act, but it didn't sound as though it was from lack of trying.

The headmistress didn't quite sigh, but I could tell from the way she let out a breath that she was nearly as frustrated by the situation as I. "As much as I can. It would give too much away to sit in on your classes on a regular basis, and so I've been attempting to gather information by other means."

"I'm sorry I couldn't get that box of Mundane devices," I said, my tone glum. "If I'd known you were only waiting for that kind of evidence to prove she was cheating, I would have punched her in the nose and run with it."

That declaration made the smile return to the headmistress's face. "I'm afraid I can't condone violence," she said. "It's enough to know you saw those things. I must confess that I'm rather at a loss as to what Mona could have done with them, though."

"You went back to look?" I asked, somewhat surprised she'd take such a liberty.

"Of course I did," Miss Primm replied. "I wouldn't be doing my job if I hadn't attempted to follow up and confirm what you'd tried to tell me. But the box has disappeared from her room, and if she's hidden it somewhere on the grounds, she's done a very good job of it, I'm afraid."

This was news I hadn't wanted to hear. Too bad Mona was too cunning for her own good. "Thank you for telling me this," I said.

The headmistress inclined her head slightly. "I know you were trying to do the right thing, Callie. Your instincts are good, even if your execution isn't always what you intend it to be. For now, it's best if you focus on your studies, however, and let me take care of the issue with Mona McGee."

"What about her father?" I asked. "If he's helping her, that's against all the codes of DOME, isn't it?"

"Yes, it is," Miss Primm replied. Her expression was almost too neutral, as if she was doing her best to prevent me from speculating as to what her true thoughts on the subject might be...not that it was terribly difficult to guess. "But again, I'll have to ask you to let me handle this. I don't want you getting involved in anything that might put you in danger."

I hadn't even thought I might be putting myself in harm's way by investigating Mona's shenanigans. "Do you really think that's a possibility?"

For a long moment, Miss Primm didn't respond. Her mouth tightened slightly, and then she said, "Yes, unfortunately. If Mona's father truly is helping her, then he's not only putting his career at risk. He's endangering his entire family, for if the Council of Magical Affairs discovers that he's violated his oath by importing Mundane artifacts and using them to illegally help his daughter cheat her way through school, then they will all be exiled, including Mona's mother and her younger brother, even if they might be blameless."

Somehow, it surprised me to hear that Mona had a sibling. I'd never heard her speak of him. Then again, it wasn't as though the two of us were in the habit of exchanging confidences, and so I suppose it wasn't so odd for me to have thought of her as an only child.

"But that's enough of that," Miss Primm went on. "You need to return to class, and I have my own business to attend to. For now, just focus on getting through your second year, and let me deal with the problem of Mona McGee."

Her tone was firm, and I knew there was no point in protesting, in saying that I wanted to help—even if I didn't know quite how. So I nodded and said, "Of course, Miss Primm."

Even as I made that promise, however, I didn't know whether I would be able to keep it.

Naturally, Juno wanted to know why Miss Primm had pulled me out of class. I told her as much as I could about my conversation with the headmistress—namely, that she wanted to congratulate me on my novel spell-craft and assure me it was fine to continue in that vein—but of course I couldn't say anything of what she'd told me about Mona and her family. Although Miss Primm hadn't come out and said so directly, I knew that she'd intended our comments to be kept between the two of us, and I wouldn't betray her trust.

Juno seemed unconvinced by my story. "You were gone an awfully long time just to get some congratulations," she said with a twist of a peach-glossed lip.

"Well, Miss Primm wanted to talk to me

about my magic," I replied. "She wanted to make sure I knew it was just fine for me to use my magic in the way I'd figured out how to make it work, and that I didn't have to worry about trying to get it to fit with the way I'd been taught to use magic in the past."

"I suppose that was nice of her," Juno said, although I could see she thought there were still some pieces missing from my story, even if she'd realized there was no point in pressing me on the subject. Then she sighed. She was lying on her bed, chin in her hands, and seemed out of sorts.

"What's the matter?" I inquired.

"Oh, I don't know," she replied, then let out a huff of a breath, her mouth pursing slightly. "It's just that...now it all seems so easy for you. You're going to ace everything while the rest of us are just poking along."

"I doubt that's going to happen," I said. I'd been sitting cross-legged on my own bed, but I got up then and went to the window to look outside. There honestly wasn't much to see; the light lingered a long time at that season, but the gardens were unoccupied. Most likely, everyone was inside studying. Our final exams were still more than a month away, but Abigail Andrews' absence served as a stark reminder that we all needed to apply ourselves if we didn't want to meet the same fate. "I'm still going to have to study like mad to pass History of Magic, and just because I've figured out a few things which will help me in Intermediate Spells, that doesn't mean getting through Potions and Kitchen Magic will be easy."

Juno didn't answer right away, but only continued to lie there, chin still resting on her balled-up fists. At last she said, "Maybe. I suppose I'm just crabby because we have a whole month more of studying ahead of us."

"That's better than having to worry about another trial," I pointed out, and she lifted an eyebrow.

"Maybe. Or maybe not. You sure made short work of the last one—maybe it would be a good thing to have the chance to earn some more points."

Clearly, she thought I was now some kind of crack spell-caster. I certainly wouldn't go so far as to say that. It was more than luck, true, and yet I wasn't a hundred-percent sure that hers—or Miss Primm's—faith in me wasn't misplaced.

However, I didn't feel like getting into an argument, so I only shrugged and said, "Well, it doesn't matter one way or another, because there won't be any more trials. Just a bunch of tests."

"And, thank the Source, a picnic wedged in there in July so the month isn't an utter wasteland of studying and nothing else." Juno sat up then, assuming a cross-legged position similar to mine. "Although one day of fun can't really make up for all the work we'll have to do."

"It's better than nothing," I said.

"I know." Her expression turned sly. "And now it looks as though you're one of Miss Primm's favorites, and so you won't have to worry about being under house arrest for this one."

About all I could do was nod. I certainly couldn't tell her that the headmistress had known all about my invisible escapade and had decided to let it go, for reasons that still seemed rather muddy to me. Perhaps it was only that she'd been forced to punish me for sneaking into Mona's room, despite secretly sympathizing with my reasons for doing so.

"As long as I stay out of trouble in the meantime," I said, and Juno grinned.

"Which is always tricky for you, I know. But you can't break into Mona's room again, and there don't seem to be many other opportunities for getting to the bottom of her tricks, so I suppose we'll just have to go along and pretend that everything's hunky-dory."

"No, I can't think of what else to do about Mona," I responded, even if that wasn't precisely the truth. Or rather, I hadn't quite given up on the notion of somehow exposing the real reason for her success in Intermediate Spells, even if I hadn't yet been able to come up with a plan for how I might achieve such a goal. "So I suppose I have no choice but to behave myself."

Juno chuckled at that comment, and soon enough we moved on to a discussion of the upcoming picnic, and whether jeans would be fine for the occasion, or whether she should write her parents to see if they'd send her a new summer dress. More than once, I'd pondered how in the world she would ever manage to get her wardrobe stuffed in her suitcase when our tenure at Miss Primm's ended, since she'd added so many new pieces of clothing since starting here, but perhaps she would simply ask her parents to send her another suitcase. Surely the rules couldn't be as strict for people who were departing the academy as they were for those who were coming here for the first and only time.

But for all our light chatter, I kept wondering if, despite what the headmistress had said, I might be able to find a way to expose Mona McGee for the fraud she truly was.

* * *

DESPITE MY PREOCCUPATION, I COULDN'T allow my mind to be completely consumed with Mona's transgressions. I knew I had to focus on the upcoming examinations. True, we had a bit more padding this year, thanks to winning two of the trials instead of only one, and yet I couldn't rely only on those extra points to see me through. There was a great deal of studying involved, and more than once I wondered if the facts I'd been cramming in my brain were going to start leaking out my ears, since it was getting so crowded in there.

One thing that did help was taking my newfound illumination about how magic worked for me and applying it to all sorts of enchantments in Intermediate Spells—and in Potions and Kitchen Magic as well, which worked out better than I'd hoped. It appeared that both Professor Hendricks and Professor Cauley were pleased with me, which was certainly a better state of affairs than had existed at the beginning of the academic year.

I even did my best to teach my technique to Celeste and Helen and Juno, with varying results. Helen couldn't seem to quite grasp what I was trying to explain, and Celeste tended to want to discuss every fine point until what I was doing no longer made any sense even to me. Juno did the best of everyone, probably because she was a fly-by-the-seat-of-her-pants sort of person anyway, and so this kind of intuitive spell-work appeared to suit her.

All in all, though, the whole lot of us were

cranky and anxious by the time the day of the picnic rolled around in mid-July. I'd begun to wonder if even a day off in the sun would be enough to put us to rights, but as soon as I saw Lochlan's smile when he alighted from his car, it was as if all the world's cares had been lifted from my shoulders.

Juno and Celeste and Helen also looked pleased to see their partners, and the whole group of us had a pleasant time together in the academy's gardens. We ate and laughed and talked about nothing of much consequence—a welcome relief—but after we were done with our picnic lunch, we all split apart into our respective couples so we could have some alone time.

Lochlan and I wandered off toward the woods, both of us agreeing that we would like some shade after eating a meal out in the open with no shelter from the bright sun overhead. Rather than head to our favorite clearing, however, we rambled for a bit with no clear destination in mind. To be honest, I was so glad to be with him, I didn't care much what we did, as long as we were together.

Eventually, though, we decided to stop for a moment and take a seat on a fallen log. "Any Mona developments?" he asked out of the blue.

Or perhaps the question wasn't completely unexpected. I hadn't brought up the topic around

the others, for obvious reasons, but I knew
Lochlan had to be wondering what I'd been up to
during the time we'd been apart. We'd written, of
course, but those letters were by necessity quite
circumspect in nature, since I could never be
entirely certain who might be reading them.

"Not really," I said. "That is, Miss Primm has
her own suspicions, but she can't do anything
without some solid evidence to back her up, and
she hasn't had any more luck finding that evidence
than I have."

Lochlan appeared somewhat startled by my
comment. "You're working with Miss Primm on
this?"

"Not really," I replied. "She confided in me,
just a little, but she also said the most important
thing was for me to study hard and pass this year's
examinations, and to let her worry about Mona
and whether her father is helping her."

"A wise bit of advice," Lochlan said. "It's probably best to let it alone for now."

Why did I get the feeling that everyone was less
worried about Mona's machinations than they
should be? Was the problem me? Did I have an
over-developed sense of justice...or was I inventing
the whole thing because I simply didn't like the girl?

"I don't have much choice but to leave it
alone, do I?" I responded, knowing even as I

spoke that I sounded positively waspish. Before Lochlan could reply, I went on, "I'm sorry. I think this whole situation has made me much too crabby. I know I should just let Miss Primm worry about it. That's her job, after all."

"Yes, it is," he said. To my relief, he didn't appear annoyed with me, despite how snappish I was being. If anything, he looked worried, as though he thought I was expending far too much mental energy on Mona McGee. "I'm not saying that you mustn't be frustrated, but sometimes it's best to know when to leave something alone for a bit."

He was probably right. At the same time, I hated leaving something unfinished like this. Even if walking away was perhaps the wiser thing to do, I didn't want to admit defeat where Mona was concerned. If she somehow managed to get away with her cheating and suffer absolutely no consequences for her deceit—except being able to graduate on false pretenses—then it would feel as though the universe had failed me on a fundamental level.

"I suppose so," I replied. To change the subject, I asked, "How's your prep going?"

The grimace he gave me in response to my question was the only answer I needed. However, he said, "As well as can be expected—which basically means I don't think I am going to flunk. It'll be close, though."

"'Close' is all you need," I told him, doing my best to be encouraging. "Once we're out the other side of this, no one is going to ask where we were ranked in our class. All the world cares about is whether we graduate or not."

And thank goodness for that. I knew I would have been even more anxious about my upcoming exams if I'd known my entire future rested on my ranking once those tests were over. But it was enough to be able to say you had graduated from Miss Primm's academy—or from Master Marco's school—and leave it at that.

Of course, graduation day was still an entire year in the future. Much closer were the second-year finals.

My words appeared to have reassured Lochlan, because he gave me one of those sunny smiles I loved so much and said, "That's true. I look forward to the day when I can be the Earl of Dundee's mediocre son and nothing more."

"There is absolutely nothing mediocre about you," I said fiercely. I hated it when he talked about himself like that, as though he was some sort of bumbling fool who just barely managed to stumble his way through life. Perhaps his magical skills weren't as strong as they could be, but he was kind and smart and a good friend. All that meant a great deal more to me than the ability to cast a flawless spell.

"I think you might be a little biased," he replied, still smiling.

"Perhaps," I said. "That doesn't mean I'm not right."

He took my hands then, his fingers warm as they wrapped themselves around mine. Although his mouth was still curved upward, something in his expression felt far more serious than it had been a moment earlier.

"I'm going to make sure I graduate," he said earnestly. "Because I want to make sure I stay here in this world with you. I know it may be early to be talking about this, but I have to know. Callie, do you want us to be together when this is all over?"

Was he asking what I thought he was asking? I didn't know whether I should read too much into his question. After all, we were both only twenty, which most people would have said was far too young to be making momentous decisions that would affect us for the rest of our lives.

And yet....

"Yes," I said, with barely a pause. "I can't say I know for sure what's going to happen, but one thing I do know is that I want you in my life."

He bent and kissed me then, his embrace as warm and welcome as the sun shining down overhead. I was acutely aware of him, of the faintly woodsy scent that I guessed was his shaving soap, the way his bit of stubble scratched against my cheek. It felt so right to be in his arms, I couldn't think of a future that didn't include him in it.

When he pulled away, his expression was deadly serious. "Then we'll both make sure to graduate, and then we can decide what we want to do after that." A pause, and he went on, "I do hate that we're stuck here away from everything. I wish I could take you home to meet my parents."

He really was deadly serious. Then again, we'd been seeing one another for a year and a half. If we'd been in the outside world, most would have thought we were well past the time when we should have been introduced to our respective families.

"They won't mind that you've taken up with an Englishwoman?" I asked, only partly teasing. Lochlan didn't talk about his father very much, but the few things he'd said had made it sound as if the man took his position as the Earl of Dundee quite seriously. Somehow I didn't think he'd be too happy to hear that his eldest son was planning on polluting the Abernathy bloodline with my much more humble English origins.

Lochlan's expression relaxed at once. "Actually, my mother is English. So my father can't give me too much grief about that aspect of the situation."

This revelation put an entirely different spin on things. "Well," I said lightly, "we can make plans for me to go visit your family in Scotland once we've graduated. It will be something to look forward to."

"One of many things," he replied, a certain warmth in his gaze telling me exactly what he was thinking of.

My cheeks turned hot as I blushed. I hoped Lochlan would think my flush was only due to the July sun and nothing more, but I couldn't know for sure. We'd kissed many times but hadn't done anything more than that, mostly because the only occasions when we could be truly private were when we were outdoors such as this, and it didn't seem safe to do anything more than kiss when there was the possibility that we could be stumbled upon at any moment. While I'd told myself I didn't mind waiting until we had safely graduated, it was times like these that I was reminded how much attending these remedial magical schools had prevented us from living our lives the way we should have.

"Yes," I said. I certainly didn't want him to think I was reluctant. It was more that we simply hadn't had the opportunity.

He reached over and took my hand. No words, but I could tell from the way he gently squeezed my fingers that he was glad we'd come to an agreement, even if no formal words had been spoken. The most important thing was that we both knew what we wanted from the future.

Now we just had to make sure we safely reached that future.

CHAPTER 12
FAMILIAR TROUBLES

The rest of July passed in a flurry of studying and practicums in both Intermediate Spells and Potions and Kitchen Magic. We were given permission to practice certain spells outside the classroom, as long as we didn't go beyond the list of recommended enchantments to work, and as long as we only cast those spells outdoors where there was less chance of harm coming to either the people in our immediate area or to the gracious manor house that housed the academy.

These restrictions were fine by me; with all the studying we were doing, it felt wonderful to have an excuse to be outside, even if it was only to engage in more spell-work. Still, it was through this practice that I finally felt as though I was making some headway in casting charms of protection, and both Celeste and Juno managed to perfect their growth spells. Even Helen surprised us all by throwing a miniature fireball, one that extinguished itself as soon as it hit the large rock where she'd been aiming the glowing sphere.

"Nice," Juno remarked as she bent down to look more closely at the char marks the fireball had left on the rock. "That could come in handy someday."

"Oh, I don't know," Helen replied, blushing slightly. "I mean, I don't see why I would ever need to throw fire at someone. But it did look impressive, didn't it?"

"Very," I said. "And I agree with Juno. You know, tossing one of those fireballs at Mona's team during football would definitely put them off their stride."

Celeste shook her head. "And be grounds for expulsion, I would imagine. You know we're not allowed to use offensive magic against other students."

Yes, I knew that as well as anyone else. Still, it had been fun to fantasize for a moment about doing something that would knock Miss McGee and her cronies off balance, if even for a bit. I shrugged, saying, "It might help for them just to know what Helen's capable of. I noticed one of them spying on us a few minutes ago."

"You did?" Helen said, throwing a worried look over her shoulder, as if she feared either Mona or one of her cronies was lurking behind a nearby tree.

"Don't worry—they're long gone," I replied, which wasn't a false reassurance. Brenda Copperpot had been pretending to merely be passing by on the walkway a few yards off, using the hedge as cover. However, I'd noticed the flash of her white shirt right away, although she'd hurried off the second I'd sent a narrow-eyed glare in her direction. "But they were definitely paying attention, which could only be a good thing. It's about time they figured out we're a force to be reckoned with."

Even Celeste nodded at that statement. While she sometimes annoyed me with her strict adherence to the academy's rules and regulations, I knew she was just as tired of Mona and her gang as the rest of us. If knowing that even shy, quiet Helen was capable of throwing a fireball on occasion made Mona just the slightest bit less irritating, I would look on that as a win for all of us.

"Still," Helen said, "I truly hope that Professor Hendricks won't ask me to cast that spell in class. It went well enough here, but I could just see my fireball going off course and blowing a hole in the wall or lighting someone's desk on fire."

"Well, if that happens, the professor will fix

it," Juno assured her. "You wouldn't get full points, but you'd still get some points for manifesting the thing."

Yes, thank the Source that partial credit was a thing in our second year. It might be enough to keep any one of us from failing outright. Between that and our extra credit from winning two trials, we were probably in a better spot than we'd been the year before.

Not that I planned to let my guard down. The promises Lochlan and I had made to one another only underscored the importance of passing all my exams this year, and doing the same thing again a year from now. Only then would I truly be free to start a life with him.

Once again, the schedule for the final exams didn't match our daily class schedule, and so our first exam was in Physical Activities. This year, we were allowed to choose which activity we wanted to be tested in, and so, while some girls chose to do the obstacle course all over again, others of us opted to perform a modest challenge of the riding skills we'd developed over the course of the year. I thought that trotting on a horse around a ring and taking my mount over a series of very small jumps was infinitely preferable to hanging from ropes and scaling walls, and so I chose to ride.

Luckily, the horse I was given for the test was one I'd ridden many times before, a sweet little sorrel mare named Strawberry, and so I didn't have any problem guiding her through the course Professor Crenshaw had set up. After I completed the final jump, I guided Strawberry back to the paddock gate where the professor waited, then dismounted.

"Very good, Callie," she said. "Full marks."

I beamed, relieved that I'd made it through my first examination with little effort. Helen and Celeste also acquitted themselves well.

Juno had decided to perform the obstacle course instead, saying she knew she would do better at that than attempting to ride. It was true that she wasn't a very good horsewoman, and so sticking with something she knew she excelled at, rather than risking being thrown—as she'd been several times before—seemed like the wisest course of action. She came off the obstacle course looking sweaty and tired, but triumphant.

"Full points," she announced, as she pulled her hair out of the elastic band that had held it out of the way and allowed her exuberant curls to bounce free. "Not that I expected anything less, but it's always nice to go into my next test knowing I don't have to make up for ground I've already lost."

Since we were all in a similar situation, we agreed it was definitely preferable. After that, we headed back to our rooms to get out of our sweaty

P.A. clothing and into our school uniforms. Although it was a warm day, I put on my cardigan, as the next test would be in Working With Familiars, and Flo and Sam much preferred to ride in my pockets rather than hang on to the much more precarious perch my shoulders provided.

We all met up in the hallway—Celeste's Siamese cat Mignon walked along just behind her, while Helen had her banty rooster Ajax tucked under one arm and Fred rode on Juno's shoulder —and headed out to the conservatory. This was another test I wasn't too worried about, since Flo and Sam had acquitted themselves beautifully all year and I didn't think I would have any trouble with them...unless Professor Hamilton came up with something particularly devious.

As it turned out, the task Professor Hamilton gave us wasn't terribly difficult. She handed each of us students a card with a picture of a flower on it, and we were supposed to show that picture to our familiars and have them seek out the flower in the conservatory and bring it back to us. Each flower was different, and so there was little risk of one girl's familiar fetching someone else's bloom.

Celeste was called first, and was given a card with a tiger lily on it. She bent down and showed it to Mignon, who seemed utterly bored by the proceedings but nevertheless headed off into the depths of the conservatory, tail flicking slightly. We were all dead silent as we waited for the cat's return, which seemed to take much longer than it should.

Eventually, however, the cat reappeared, jeweled collar gleaming, a spotted lily clutched in her teeth. At once, Celeste bent and praised her familiar, and went over to Professor Hamilton, lily clutched in her hand.

"Excellent," the professor said, making a notation in the book she carried. "Full points."

Looking infinitely relieved, Celeste picked up Mignon and took her place between Juno and me. To Juno's other side, Helen appeared worried, teeth nibbling at her lower lip. All through the year, her little rooster had only been able to accomplish his tasks about half the time, and so I could see why she might be nervous. On the surface, this particular challenge didn't seem too difficult, and yet Ajax had botched equally simple tests before this.

Philippa was called next, to my relief. If she was worried, she showed absolutely no sign of it. Professor Hamilton gave her a picture of a pansy, brilliant in purple and gold, and Philippa's squirrel Mr. Butters scampered off right away, luxuriant furry tail at the ready.

It seemed as though barely a moment had passed before the squirrel returned, a pansy in the specified colors drooping from between his teeth.

"Excellent," the professor said. "Full points to you, Philippa."

And so it went. Everyone's familiars seemed to be in fine form that day—including Helen's rooster Ajax, who came back with the requested purple iris far more quickly than any of us had expected. She picked him up afterward, stroking his feathers and praising him, and he preened and let out a triumphant little crow.

And then it was Mona's turn. Professor Hamilton gave her a picture of a peony, all rosy-pink ruffles. Mona took it, mouth tight. True, the flower might be a bit unwieldy for her rat, but surely even he should be able to manage such a simple task.

When she put him down on the ground, however, he sat there for a moment, looking about in bewilderment, as if he didn't know quite what to do. Frowning, she bent down and showed him the picture of the flower again, even as one hand lingered in the pocket of her cardigan.

Because I'd been watching for such a thing, my eyes at once narrowed in suspicion. I didn't know what she was doing, but clearly, it had some effect on poor Silas the rat, as he gave a squeak that almost sounded as if he was in pain. His tail waved back and forth in agitation, and then he squeaked again before bounding off into the conservatory.

She stood back up, one corner of her mouth lifted in a faint smirk. As soon as she saw me looking at her, however, the smirk disappeared, and she assumed a studiedly neutral expression. Since all of my classmates were staring off into the greenery, watching for Silas' return, I doubted that anyone else had noticed the sinister smile his mistress had been wearing.

And return the rat did, with a large, showy pink peony clutched in his tiny mouth. He appeared relieved beyond measure when Mona took it from him, and wearily hopped up into her pocket—the other one, not the pocket where she'd placed her hand.

"Well done," Professor Hamilton said. "Full points to you and Silas, Mona."

"Thank you, professor," she replied, all but simpering. "We've been practicing a lot."

"Your practice appears to have paid off." Professor Hamilton paused then and glanced over at me. "Callie, it's your turn."

I stepped forward. The professor pulled a card from the few remaining in the stack she held. It showed a picture of a red gladiolus, tall and stately.

"I thought I should give you something that

both your familiars would have to work together to carry," she said.

Even working together, carrying something that size would be a challenge for the two gerbils. Irritation flashed through me, even though I told myself that it was only fair for Professor Hamilton to give me a task which would make Flo and Sam work as a proper team. They poked their noses out of their pockets, and I showed them the card.

See this one? I thought. *So bright and tall? Go find one of these and bring it back to me.*

At once, they jumped out of my pockets and disappeared into the lush plants that crowded the conservatory. I knew I'd seen those flowers blooming off to one side, and wished I'd told them where to look. However, our connection was probably strong enough that they knew even without my direct input.

Still, it was hard to stand there and wait…and wait…especially since everyone else had fared so well in their tests so far. Quite possibly, Flotsam and Jetsam weren't taking any longer than Helen's rooster or even Mona's rat, but it felt as though eons were crawling by.

Eventually, though, a flash of red appeared on one of the conservatory's walkways, and the two gerbils appeared, struggling their way along under their burden. I wanted to go and take the flower from them, but made myself wait until they were at my feet. Only then did I reach down and lift the gladiolus from their tiny jaws, and hold it up for everyone to see.

"Very well done," Professor Hamilton said. "Full marks to you, Callie."

I sagged in relief, and bent down and picked up Flo and Sam so I could put them in my pocket. Usually, they would have jumped, but I didn't want to have them make the effort after their exertions in getting the gladiolus to me.

After that, Professor Hamilton went through the remainder of the class. Missy Cantu's ferret Rosalie scampered off and was back with her requested yellow rose so quickly, we barely had time to blink. Missy, too, was given full marks, and then we were let go to have our lunch and the rest of the afternoon off.

My little group had barely sat down with our picnic lunches before I said, "Mona was at it again. She had her hand in her pocket as she was giving Silas his instructions. I don't know what she was doing, exactly, but it seemed to be hurting the poor thing."

"Why would she be hurting him?" Helen asked. "How would that get him to do what she wanted?"

Juno shot her a pitying look, as if she couldn't quite believe anyone could be so naïve. "People have been abusing animals for thousands of years to train them. That's how they used to get elephants and lions to do tricks before circuses were outlawed."

"Abusing your familiar is horrible," Celeste said, her full mouth tight with distaste. "It's betraying a sacred trust."

I understood precisely what she meant. Familiars were family. And yet, if Mona didn't have any real magic, then she would never have experienced a true bond with Silas, and quite possibly wouldn't feel as moved to take good care of him. If hurting the rat meant she could finally get him to perform a necessary task and pass her final exam, then I doubted she would scruple at stooping to such behavior to advance to her third and final year at the academy.

"Well, it's Mona McGee we're talking about," I said. "I wouldn't put anything past her."

No one replied to that comment, probably because all my friends knew I was right. As we sat there in uncomfortable silence, I wondered if there was some way I could figure out what Mona had used to make Silas obey her. If it was another piece of forbidden Mundane technology, it might finally be the bit of evidence I could give Miss Primm to show that Mona truly was guilty of cheating to stay in school.

In fact, a plan began to form in my head. I'd noticed how Mona had been late arriving for lunch and had emerged from the building with her cardigan gone, as though she'd known it was far too hot to wear the thing out of doors but hadn't wanted to take the risk of simply removing it and tying it around her waist, in case whatever gadget she'd used to control Silas might have fallen out. She was currently sitting with her cronies, laughing and talking.

Which meant no one was in her room, or anywhere nearby.

"It's hot," I said abruptly. "I'm going to take my cardigan up to my room. Be back in a moment."

Juno shot me a puzzled glance. "Just take it off and put it on the bench or something. You don't need to go all the way to our room just for that."

"No, it's better to just get rid of it," I replied. "I won't need Flo and Sam with me after this anyway. I might as well put them in their cage and give them a treat."

One eyebrow lifted, but Juno didn't argue, only reached for an apple slice and bit it in half. I took her silence as permission to leave, and so I got up from where I sat and hurried into the school building, casting a sideways look at Mona and her friends as I left. Her back was partially to me, and so I didn't think she even noticed my departure.

Perfect. As soon as I was inside—and as soon

as I'd determined that no one else was about—I turned invisible and quickly made my way up the staircase. From there, I hastened down the hallway to Mona's room. A quick pause to make sure no one was anywhere nearby, and I put my hand on the doorknob.

It was locked. What in the world?

None of the students' rooms had locks. Some of us had grumbled about privacy, but really, we'd given up so many rights while attending the academy that not being able to lock a door was fairly far down my list of grievances. And since none of the professors had ever done anything so crass as to barge into someone's room without knocking and waiting first, there really wasn't much to complain about.

Because there wasn't a physical lock on the door—at least, not one I could see—that made me think Philippa must have cast a charm of some sort on it. This sort of thing was forbidden, but I doubted either Mona or her roommate were too worried about the rules. With them, it was all about not getting caught.

Well, if a spell was keeping the door locked, then that meant there must be some kind of counter-spell to unlock it. In my case, I didn't require anything as complicated as a counter-spell, however…not with the way I'd recently learned to work magic. I closed my eyes and breathed in, and imagined the click of the lock as it disengaged, and how it would look when the door swung inward.

A second later, that was exactly what happened.

I let out a breath, opened my eyes, and sent another quick glance up and down the corridor. No one was about, but I knew that situation wouldn't last indefinitely. Sooner rather than later, everyone would finish their lunch, and although I guessed a large number would wish to remain outside to enjoy the warm weather, there would still be those who wanted to come back inside to do their studying in their rooms, or perhaps in the library.

Which meant I didn't have a moment to lose.

I slipped inside Mona's room and shut the door, and was greeted by the same mess I'd seen the first time I'd gained illegal entry to the place. This time, however, I wasn't worried about the clutter. Instead, my gaze was drawn immediately to a bright red cardigan draped over the back of a chair.

Perfect.

After hurrying over to it, I stuck my hand in the cardigan's right pocket—the same pocket where Mona had secreted whatever gadget she'd used to force Silas into obeying her commands. My fingers closed around a hard, cylindrical object, obviously metal, as it was cool to the touch.

I pulled it out but didn't bother to inspect it closely. That would come later. For now, I just deposited the device in the pocket that Flo and Sam weren't currently occupying, then let myself back out.

However, I couldn't allow myself to savor the triumph, not when I'd just realized I needed to somehow get the locking charm back in place, or Mona and Philippa would surely know that someone had been inside their room. And although I'd never cast that sort of spell, I told myself all I needed to do was visualize the door being locked, and it should take care of itself.

Only when I put my hand on the knob, it turned easily. So much for my quick-and-dirty method of spell-casting.

From down the corridor came the sound of voices and feet slapping on the hardwood stairs.

Oh, no.

Desperate, I shut my eyes and imagined Philippa casting a charm on the door so it wouldn't unlock except at her command. Obviously, she must have been the one who'd cast the spell, since Mona had no magic of her own.

This time when I tried to twist the doorknob, it wouldn't turn. I let out a quick breath of relief and then hurried down the hallway to the room I shared with Juno, and closed the door behind me. Not a moment too soon, because I heard footsteps going past only a few seconds after I'd reached my current place of refuge.

It was enough, though.

I pulled out the device to inspect it, even as Flo and Sam scampered out of my other pocket and jumped onto the dresser where their cage was located. They immediately began stuffing their faces on the feed in the cage's tray, and I experienced a pang of guilt. I really should have brought them back here immediately after class, rather than thinking it would be all right to make them wait until I was done with lunch. Carrying that gladiolus must have been exhausting.

But if I'd done that, I wouldn't have had an excuse to come back inside now...and I wouldn't be holding the object I'd just taken from Mona's room.

It appeared very simple. It had two buttons, one of which glowed red when I pushed it. However, it didn't seem to do anything more than that.

Except...had that been a couple of irritated squeaks coming from inside Flo and Sam's cage?

I turned back toward them, and pushed the button on the device again. At once, my two gerbils seemed to cringe, and let out more of those annoyed squeals.

For a long moment, I stared down at the device. I hadn't heard anything, but it seemed to me that it must emit some kind of sound that only rodents could hear, something that made them react in pain.

Something Mona could use to control poor Silas and get him to do her bidding.

This was the incontrovertible proof I needed to show that she truly was using Mundane devices to get ahead at the academy.

Because it would have looked conspicuous to put my cardigan back on, I instead slipped the device up my sleeve and made sure the cuff was buttoned securely so the strange little silvery object wouldn't slide out. After that, I went back out into the hallway, offering a few casual "hello"s to the girls I passed before descending the staircase.

From there, it didn't take long for me to get to Miss Primm's office. At the doorway, I hesitated for a moment. What if she wasn't there? Then I would have to find a place to hide the device until I could safely give it to her. She came and went from Master Marco's school so often these days, I thought it a distinct possibility that she might not be in her office, or even on the school grounds. And—

The door opened, and she looked out at me, expression not surprised at all. "Come in, Callie."

"How—how did you know I was here?" I blurted.

Her mouth lifted in a half-smile. "Because it's my business to know these things. Come inside, please."

She stepped out of the way, and I entered her office. As soon as I was inside, she shut the door.

"It must be something important," she said, still smiling.

In response, I unbuttoned my cuff and slid out the gadget I'd taken from Mona's room. "I found this. I think Mona was using it to control her familiar. Some kind of painful sound, I think, although I don't know for absolutely sure."

Miss Primm took the object from me, her elegantly arched brows drawing together as she appeared to study it closely. "How were you able to get this away from Mona?"

Lying didn't seem like a very good idea, and so I said simply, "I turned invisible and took it from her room while she was having lunch."

"Callie—" the headmistress said in warning tones.

"Oh, I know," I said quickly. "I suppose it was wrong. But I knew she'd done something to that poor rat of hers, because her hand was in her cardigan pocket the whole time during our Working With Familiars final, just as it always is whenever she's using a Mundane device. So I went to take a look." I paused there before adding, "You did tell me that you couldn't do anything about Mona until you had evidence. Well, here's some evidence."

"That it is," she replied. For a moment, she was quiet, studying the device she held. "Master Marco has made a study of Mundane technology, so I'll take it to him and see whether he agrees with your hypothesis. From there, I'll decide what to do next."

I wasn't terribly surprised that she'd want to go to Master Marco for his advice. She did seem to take whatever opportunity she could to see him— and if he truly was an expert on Mundane devices, then he seemed like the logical person to consult.

Even so, I hated the idea of having to wait for him to weigh in. "What should I do?" I asked.

"Nothing," Miss Primm said at once. "I'm sure Mona will realize soon enough that her device is missing. You did cover your tracks, didn't you?"

"I was careful not to touch anything else, and I re-cast the locking charm on the door as I was leaving."

Her eyes narrowed. "A lock charm? That's against school rules."

"Do you really think Mona cares?" I asked.

"No, probably not." The headmistress paused there, suddenly looking tired. "Well, it isn't as if she can go around the school and ask people what happened to her device without giving away her entire game. But still, please try to avoid taking these sorts of risks from now on."

"There's no need to, is there?" I responded. "That is, I only wanted to find some evidence you could work with, and it seems I've done that."

She inclined her head and said, "Yes, you have."

But rather than seeming pleased with me, she only appeared weary still, as if she now had an additional burden she didn't quite know how to bear. However, in the next moment, she summoned another smile.

"Thank you, Callie. I know you still have a lot of studying to do, so I won't keep you from it."

The dismissal was clear, so I only nodded and let myself out, quietly closing the door to Miss Primm's office behind me.

I'd done the right thing. I only wished I felt better about it.

Juno, of course, was very happy to hear about my successful foray into espionage. On the way back up to my room, I'd decided not to say anything to Celeste and Helen, not so much because I felt I couldn't trust them, but the more people who held a secret, the less secure it became. They'd find out soon enough if the headmistress decided to take action.

"What do you think Miss Primm is going to do about that device you found?" Juno asked me later that evening, after we had gotten ready for bed and were about to retire for the night. "Do you think she's going to go to DOME?"

"I'm not sure," I said, which was only the truth.

I'd derived some satisfaction from seeing how Mona had seemed irritable and almost panicky at dinner that evening, but of course, I'd stayed as far away from her as I could. She'd shot a few suspicious looks in my direction, as was to be expected. However, since she hadn't tried to confront me, I guessed she didn't know for sure who had been behind the theft of her Mundane device—if it had even been theft at all. Most likely, she probably feared that the gadget had somehow managed to fall out of her pocket somewhere between the conservatory and her room, which left a lot of ground to cover.

But even though I knew I'd done the right thing, some of Miss Primm's malaise seemed to be catching. Perhaps it was only that I felt in limbo, unsure as to what steps the headmistress planned to take next. "That is," I went on as Juno continued to watch me, brows lifted inquiringly, "she's going to have Master Marco look at the device and see if he agrees that it was using sound in some way to control Mona's familiar, but she didn't say anything other than that. I suppose she wants to have as many facts as possible on hand before she takes any further steps."

"That makes sense," Juno said. She had her knees drawn up to her chest with her arms wrapped around them, wild hair pulled back into a loose stretchy band for the night. "I mean, I know I'd want to have all my ducks in a row before I started making any accusations. I sort of hope she waits until after the next school year starts—it would be so wonderful to watch Mona getting marched out of class in front of everyone."

While I must admit I'd harbored fantasies of that very thing happening, I was also forced to recognize that real life very rarely mirrored what we desired in our dreams. "I don't know whether she'll wait or not," I said. "It probably depends on what Master Marco tells her. And she might not want to cause any disruption, since the end of our exams is so close."

"Not close enough," Juno replied, and let out a dramatic sigh. "I've studied and studied until it feels as if my brains are pouring out of my ears, but I still don't know whether it will be enough. I kind of hate that we have both Potions and Kitchen Magic and Intermediate Spells on the same day. Not that History of Magic is a picnic, either, but at least that exam is just answering questions and not having to actually do magic."

"I know," I said. "I'm not sure if there's any real logic to it, or whether Miss Primm simply puts all the class names on slips of paper and then draws them out of a hat to make the final exam schedule. But however it works, we might as well go to sleep. We're going to need our rest for tomorrow."

"I suppose so," Juno said, sounding sulky. "I just hate days like tomorrow. Yes, I want it over with, but I also sort of want it to hang back for as long as possible."

I chuckled. "I know the feeling. But it's going to get here no matter what we do, so we might as well be as rested as possible."

She muttered her agreement, and I said, "Lights out," plunging the room into darkness.

After all, what I'd said was only the obvious truth.

Tomorrow would come soon enough.

* * *

WHEN WE ALL TROOPED INTO PROFESSOR Cauley's classroom the next morning, the following words were neatly written on the blackboard.

Choose ONE:
Night Vision
Growth
Flying

I tried not to groan, and I could tell from Juno's fierce frown that she wasn't happy with the choices, either. Because our previous final exams had been comparatively easy, I supposed we were all hoping that the Potions and Kitchen Magic final would be the proverbial walk in the park. But, judging by our one and only test question, I could tell it wasn't going to be that simple.

"Good morning, class," Professor Cauley said as she beamed at us. Her cheerful, rosy face provided absolutely no sign that she'd noted our consternation. "As you can see from the board, your final consists of only one practical application. Please select one of the potions listed on the board, gather the ingredients, brew your potion, and use it on yourself to demonstrate its efficacy. And no worries," she added with a small chuckle. "I am here to put things to rights if it turns out that your potion doesn't perform in the way you intended. You have one hour to mix your potion. After that, we will proceed to the practical phase."

Too bad we weren't doing this in teams. Helen had actually gotten quite good at making potions, and we would have had a much better chance of success if we could have leaned on her, so to speak. But clearly, the professor wasn't going to make it that easy.

I studied my options again. Night Vision sounded deceptively simple, but I knew that some of the potion's ingredients—namely, hemlock, bat claws, and feverfew—tasted positively horrible. A growth potion could get out of hand far too easily. Flight seemed the safest, if only because there wasn't too much damage one could do to oneself when falling from a height of only a dozen feet or so.

The thought crossed my mind that perhaps I

could pretend to make a flight potion and then instead use an actual enchantment to simulate the potion's effects—especially since I'd done something similar in Intermediate Spells—but I dismissed the notion almost at once. Surely Professor Cauley would have the means to detect whether a student's flight had been achieved in the manner the test demanded. Cheating in such a way seemed like a surefire way to get expelled, or at the very least, forfeit any points that might otherwise have been earned by taking the test.

Very well. I set my jaw and went to the cabinets that occupied one entire wall of the room, then gathered the necessary ingredients for the potion. All around, my classmates were doing much the same. None of them looked very happy, but Mona seemed positively thunderous, perhaps because she knew she had no way of faking the effects of any of the suggested potions, and so would flunk the test no matter what happened. There was the faint possibility that Professor Cauley would still award her a few points if the potion had been assembled in the correct order and with the correct proportions, but it wouldn't be anything close to what Mona might have earned if she'd had the necessary magic to make a potion actually work.

But I knew I needed to stop worrying about what Mona could or couldn't do. Potions was definitely the weaker of my two practicum classes, since my own odd brand of magic didn't lend itself very well to the sort of precise measurements this particular type of kitchen magic required. However, I knew I must still try my hardest. Lochlan's face flashed into my mind, and I told myself I had to do this for him, even if I didn't care whether I brewed another potion in my life after I was done at Miss Primm's.

Very well, then.

I went to the ingredients cabinets and gathered the birch bark, bee pollen, spring water, and other items required for a potion of flight. After I'd filled an assortment of flasks and vials with the necessary ingredients, I went back to my workstation and conjured a flame under the bronze bowl that waited there.

Painstakingly, I added each ingredient in what my notes said was the proper order, then slowly stirred until the liquid in the bowl reached a slow simmer. I had to stir it for three minutes clockwise and three minutes counterclockwise, and then let it grow still as I turned down the flame and allowed it to cool.

What was left was a shimmering blue-green liquid, just slightly viscous. I ladled it into a flask and attached a neatly lettered label, because Professor Cauley was adamant that we be as precise with our potions as possible.

All around me, my classmates were doing much the same thing with their own potions. Juno, who had the workstation next to mine, apparently had decided to attempt the night vision elixir, since the liquid she placed in her flask was a deep, deep purple, nearly black. Helen's, on the other hand, was bright green, apparently the potion of growth. Since Celeste was working on the other side of Helen, I couldn't see her potion clearly, although I guessed I'd be able to tell which one she'd chosen just as soon as she tested it on herself.

"Time, everyone," Professor Cauley said. "Instead of doing this in alphabetical order, I'll group you according to the potions you made. Hands of everyone who chose the night vision potion."

The hands of more than half the classroom went up, Juno's and Celeste's included…as well as Mona McGee's. Apparently, more people were willing to make something that tasted horrible if the risk of taking the potion was much lower.

"Very good," the professor said. "Elixir of growth?"

Helen and Philippa and a handful of others raised their hands. I glanced around the room, made a quick mental calculation, and swallowed.

"Potion of flight?"

I reluctantly raised my hand…the only person

to raise her hand. Right then, I wanted to kick myself. Why hadn't I taken the easy path and made myself a batch of that night vision sludge? It couldn't taste *that* bad, could it?

"Very courageous of you," Professor Cauley remarked, then added, in a brisker tone, "We'll start with the night vision group, since there are so many of you. Everyone, make sure you stay at your workstations, especially if you haven't made this particular elixir. It's about to get very dark in here."

Immediately after she finished speaking, the room went utterly dark—so pitch black that I couldn't even see my hand when I waved it in front of my face.

"Now, then," the professor went on. "Juno Hightower. What am I holding in my hand?"

Juno replied, voice confident, "A pocket watch."

"Excellent," Professor Cauley said. "Full points."

From there, she went through the rest of the night vision group. Only Louise Langford faltered, saying that the professor held a pencil in her hand when it was actually a willow twig.

Then Professor Cauley said, "Mona McGee? What do I have in my hand?"

"A compass," Mona replied at once, sounding

smug. "A compass for direction," she clarified. "Not the kind you use to draw circles."

"Very good," the professor said. "Full points."

It was probably a good thing the classroom was pitch black, because I had a feeling that I was looking completely gobsmacked. How in the world could Mona have known that? I would have sworn she didn't have enough magic to create a halfway effective potion, let alone one that had allowed her to see perfectly in the dark. Was this some sort of Mundane technology that gave her night vision? I supposed that was possible, but shouldn't have Professor Cauley been able to tell Mona was using some kind of gadget?

Perhaps, I thought. *Or perhaps not. It's possible that the professor didn't see the need to take a potion, since she already knew what she was holding. If that's the case, she wouldn't be able to see Mona any better than I can.*

And if Mona had used a gadget to imitate the effects of a night-vision potion, then all her ire earlier must have been only an act, one she'd employed to make anyone watching her believe she didn't have a chance of passing this particular test.

I didn't have time to speculate further, because the classroom suddenly became its usual brightly lit self. If Mona had been using some kind of Mundane device, it was now safely stowed away.

From there, the professor moved on to the students who'd created growth elixirs for themselves. Helen actually did quite well, blowing herself up to double her size—an effect that only lasted for a moment, when she shrank back to her regular petite stature.

"It would have been nice if it had lasted longer," Professor Cauley commented. "However, since I didn't specify a duration, you've earned full points for this examination."

Helen flushed bright pink, and I released a small breath in relief. I'd been worried that she wouldn't be able to pull it off, but it seemed my fears had been for nothing.

Philippa Carmody didn't fare quite as well, since her potion made her head swell to three times its usual size while the rest of her body stayed the same. She had to hold on to her head, her thin neck unable to support its girth, until the professor came over and quickly cast a counter-spell that immediately returned her skull to normal.

"Partial points," was all the professor said, and Philippa nodded. She didn't look too concerned, but that was probably because her team had enough extra points on hand to easily cover the deficit.

And then Professor Cauley turned to me.

"Callie Dobkins."

I nodded, hoping I didn't look as anxious as I felt. My potion was for flight, but it seemed as though I had several dozen butterflies fluttering around in my stomach already.

Because I knew that hesitating would only make matters worse, I lifted my flask of potion and swallowed a large mouthful. It had a fresh, minty taste, not unlike mouthwash, so I thought I'd gotten that part right.

And then my body began to feel lighter and lighter, and I realized I was floating up into the air. I gave an experimental flap of my arms, and the movement propelled me up toward the ceiling.

Because I'd flown before through the means of a flying charm, the sensation wasn't completely novel. However, this time it seemed easier to move about, as though the potion itself had some sort of buoyancy that kept me floating in the air.

"Very good," Professor Cauley called up to me. "Now, come down, please."

I flapped my arms again, but all that did was push my body forward. A flare of panic went through me, although I did my best to calm myself.

"Now, Callie."

Easier said than done. No matter what I tried, I remained hovering stubbornly near the ceiling.

Several feet below me, Mona snickered, and I held back a curse.

Very well. Since the potion seemed determined to keep me stuck in midair indefinitely, I decided I would just have to use my own magic to get myself down. I imagined my body fluttering gently to the ground, the effects of the potion effectively neutralized.

Only nothing happened.

Once again, panic flared in me, this time much stronger. What if I got stuck up here indefinitely?

Echoing my thoughts, Professor Cauley asked, "Are you stuck, Callie?"

I hated to admit defeat, but I hated the thought of continuing to float there for who knows how long even more. "Erm...I think so."

Her mouth quirked slightly. "That's what I thought."

I didn't hear her speak the counter-spell, but the next thing I knew, I was drifting gently downward until my feet touched solid ground. Somehow, I managed to fight back the urge to kiss it.

"An effective potion," the professor commented. "Perhaps too effective. Partial points."

Better than nothing, I supposed. She could have decided to award me zero points. I would just have to wait until the final point tallies were posted to see if it was enough to keep me in school.

Afterward, Juno tried to cheer me up. "It did seem like a pretty decent potion," she said as we ate lunch. "And I'm sure it tasted better than mine." She grimaced.

"If we were being judged on flavor, then yes, I'm sure I would have gotten full points," I replied. "As it is, I can only hope I do better in the Intermediate Spells final."

She opened her mouth as though to give me further reassurances, then closed it again when she apparently decided it was better to let the matter go.

To my infinite relief, the final test of the year did go much better. I was able to create a glowing arc of light around me, as well as to shroud myself in darkness, thus earning full points from Professor Hendricks. Helen stumbled a bit as she attempted to create an illusion of a doorway in the wall, but the fireball she tossed from hand to hand appeared to impress even the professor.

As I'd guessed, Mona sailed through her test with ease, and her teammates fared well, too. When we all gathered outside Miss Primm's office the following day to see our marks, it was to find that everyone in the second-year class had passed, even though some, like Louise Langford, had skated through by the skin of their teeth.

I scored 698 points, not as good as my first year, but enough to save me from Mundania, and Helen and Juno and Celeste weren't far behind. Mona had managed to come out on top, no doubt in part because of her stellar performance in the Potions and Kitchen Magic final. I still hadn't figured that one out, and perhaps I never would.

But I told myself it didn't matter. I had passed, and that was the most important thing.

Now, we had two weeks of freedom to look forward to.

CHAPTER 14
THE VANISHING

This time, our summer holiday wasn't quite the novel experience the first one had been, but it still felt glorious to know that we had an entire fortnight with nothing to trouble us except minor decisions such as whether we should go riding, or rowing on the pond, or simply pack a picnic lunch and ramble to our hearts' content. Cars went back and forth from Master Marco's school to Miss Primm's academy—or vice versa—on a daily basis, although the headmaster and headmistress of those two institutions were nowhere to be seen.

"Oh, I'm quite certain they went off somewhere together," Lochlan said. That day, we'd decided to take our picnic lunch to a far edge of the estate's holdings, in a sheltered little spot shaded by beech trees and with a lovely flat expanse of grass on which to spread a blanket. We lounged there, fully determined to do absolutely nothing except allow ourselves to bask in the beauty of the day—and the joy of one another's company.

"How do you know that for sure?" I asked, then popped a grape in my mouth.

"Because it's the most sensible explanation," he said. "They both left on holiday on exactly the same day—"

"Only because the summer break starts on the same day at both schools," I broke in.

Being Lochlan, he didn't seem annoyed with me for the interruption. "True, but they didn't do that last year. That is, while they were both on holiday at roughly the same time, Master Marco didn't leave for his until we students had been on break for several days."

"Perhaps they were trying to hide their relationship last year," I suggested. To be honest, I'd only been playing devil's advocate; anyone who had two functioning eyes in their head could see there was something going on between the headmaster and the headmistress, even if they hadn't openly admitted to the relationship. "And now they clearly have decided that there isn't much point."

"No, there isn't," Lochlan replied with a grin. "And good for them. I just wonder how they're going to manage things if they decide to formalize their relationship."

"Would they, though?" I asked, somewhat dubious on the subject. "After all, there've been generations of Miss Primms running this place, but not one of them has ever gotten married. The place isn't called 'Mrs. Primm's Academy for Wayward Witches,' after all."

"I suppose that's between Miss Primm and Master Marco," Lochlan said equably. "Just because something has never been done before doesn't mean it can't happen at some point."

This comment seemed so obviously true that I didn't bother to argue the point. "I suppose we'll have to see what happens," I said. "I'm sure we'll have enough to keep us occupied during our third year that the personal lives of Master Marco and Miss Primm won't be able to take up much space in our heads."

Lochlan grimaced, even as he leaned forward to pluck a couple of grapes off the bunch that lay on the plate between us. "That's for certain. I can't say I'm much looking forward to it."

Neither was I. My score had dropped by nearly a hundred points between my first year and my second year at the academy. I simply couldn't afford another hundred-point drop at the end of my third year; that would mean I had failed just as I was nearing the finish line.

I didn't want to think about that dismal prospect, however. Those missing points had all come from my botched potion, and I would simply have to do better this coming school year. I would play it safe whenever possible, and keep my head down and do the necessary work to ensure I wouldn't be exiled.

"No," I said. "But at least we only have one year ahead of us rather than two. That does make the situation a bit easier to stomach."

He nodded. "I guess that's a good way to look at it. And I suppose that's why I enjoy being around you so much—you always try to make the best of things."

That familiar warmth fluttered in my stomach. "Well, it's easy to make the best of things when I'm with you."

My words brought a smile to his lips, and we leaned in and shared a very satisfying kiss, sweet with the juice of the grapes we'd just eaten. It felt so good to be there with him in the sunlight...so good to pretend, if only for a bit, that perfect moments such as these would go on forever.

Of course, they did not.

* * *

NONE OF MY LITTLE GROUP VIEWED THE school's traditional "first day" dinner with any trepidation, not when we'd gone through this whole thing twice before. Technically, the beginning of the term would commence the following morning, but this dinner was what kicked off the formal start of the school year.

It felt odd to think that we would now be lordly third-year students. We'd been moved to new rooms; these ones were on the top floor, and felt airier and more spacious, the furnishings a bit nicer, not so scratched by generations of previous use.

"The first thing I'm going to do when we get out of here," Juno announced as she fluffed her hair in front of the mirror, "is burn this stupid uniform. I am soooo tired of looking at it."

While I had to agree with that sentiment, I couldn't help saying, "Isn't it a bit soon to be tired of it? After all, we just spent two weeks in jeans and summer dresses."

She made a face. "You know what I mean."

"I suppose I do," I said, relenting. "And I'll be happy to join you in making a bonfire of these things. I assume wool burns well enough?"

"Only one way to find out," she said with a grin.

Well, if nothing else, I figured it would be a good test of our fire-starting skills. "It's a plan," I replied. "But first, we have to get through this next year."

Her mouth twisted. "I know. And believe me, I am *really* not looking forward to it. I feel as if we just barely squeaked by last year. If they make the third year too much harder than the second, how in the world are we supposed to graduate?"

"I don't know," I said. "But hundreds of students have managed to do that very thing, so I suppose we'll muddle through somehow. For now, I think it's enough to know that we're third-years, and all the other students will be looking at us and wondering if they'll ever manage to get where we are now."

"I like the way you think," Juno said with a grin. "I suppose we'd better get going, though. Let's collect Helen and Celeste—if we're too late, we won't get good seats, third-years or no."

This was true, and so I checked on Flo and Sam's water and food, then bade them a quick farewell as Juno and I left the room. Celeste and Helen were ready to go, and the four of us headed downstairs.

"I don't know why the third-years get stuck on the top floor," Juno grumbled as we made our descent. "There are so many more stairs to climb."

"But the view is lovely," Celeste returned, to which Juno gave a reluctant lift of her shoulders.

"I suppose. Still, it would be nice if the school could have borrowed just a little bit of Mundane technology and put in an elevator."

"How would it run without electricity?" I asked. I still didn't know all that much about how the Mundane world worked, but I knew enough to remember that a great deal of their technology was dependent on something called electricity, a mysterious force which appeared to power many of their devices.

Being Juno, she had a ready answer. "Magic, of course. We use it for everything else, don't we?"

I had to admit that was true. In our world, there were quite a few analogues of the technology used in Mundania, only magic was our electricity. Which, I suppose, begged the question as to why the school didn't have a magically powered lift. I could only surmise that the early founders of the school had decided climbing stairs built character.

We reached the ground floor and made our way to the dining room. As I'd feared, it was already quite crowded, but I'd forgotten that third-year students had some of the choicest tables set aside for their use. Because of this, the four of us were able to grab several spots at the end of a table already occupied by another group of thirds —not Mona and her cadre, thank goodness, but Louise Langford and several of her friends.

"New year, same speeches, I suppose," Louise observed.

"Probably," Juno replied. "At this point, they've pretty much said it all. Although I suppose we can always hope that Miss Primm will add even more social events to the calendar."

"Too many more, and we won't have any time to go to regular classes," Louise's friend Misty remarked.

"You say that like it's a bad thing," Juno said, and everyone laughed. By that point, even the most studious among us were getting a bit weary of the grind.

The last few professors took their seats at the head tables, and the students' tables likewise were filled by some stragglers, mostly firsts who obviously had taken some time to figure out where they were supposed to go. After that, the room quieted as we all waited for Miss Primm to make her appearance so she could give her usual welcome speech. Only after that tradition had been satisfied could we get down to the important task of eating our dinner.

And we waited...and waited. There weren't any clocks in the dining hall, but I guessed a good ten minutes must have passed. At the head table, Professor Hendricks got up from her seat, then went over to the door the instructors used to access the room and let herself out.

"What's going on?" Juno murmured to me.

I shook my head. "I don't know. Maybe Miss Primm just forgot it was time to come to dinner."

"After doing this for how many years?" she

returned, her expression and tone dubious in the extreme.

I had to admit my suggestion didn't seem like a very plausible scenario. Perhaps the headmistress had been delayed coming back from her holiday with Master Marco. Miss Primm did seem to be very good at stealth, since no one ever seemed able to note her comings and goings with any great accuracy. She simply reappeared in her office as if she'd been there all along.

During Professor Hendricks' absence, the murmur in the crowd grew louder and louder. I could see quite a few of the firsts looking around in bewilderment, as if they knew something was wrong but couldn't quite figure out what to do about it.

Well, they weren't alone in that. Surely if Miss Primm had had something happen to her on holiday which would have prevented her from returning to the academy on time, she would have sent word ahead to let her instructors know about the situation. Since Professor Hendricks had looked quite flummoxed as she got up from her seat, I had to surmise that wasn't the current situation.

After a span of moments that felt absolutely excruciating, the professor returned to the hall. Although she had never been the type of person to show much color in her cheeks, now she appeared positively ghostly. She bent and exchanged a rapid-fire volley of whispers with Professor Cauley, who also turned pale. Then she gave a reluctant nod.

Their *sotto voce* conversation completed, Professor Hendricks turned toward the watching students. Her hand shook slightly as she reached up to straighten her lapel, and then she said, "Miss Primm should have been here to welcome you to another school year. However...." Her words trailed off there, and she squared her shoulders and lifted her chin.

"There is no easy way to say this. It appears that Miss Primm is missing."

Miss Primm's School for Wayward Witches concludes in *Expelled*, the third book of the trilogy.

HEDGEWITCH FOR HIRE

(Mystery/Paranormal romance)

Grave Mistake

Social Medium

Household Demons

Perpetual Potion

Jingle Spells (December 2021)

Wandering Monsters (March 2022)

THE WITCHES OF WHEELER PARK

(Paranormal romance)

Storm Born

Thunder Road

Winds of Change

Mind Games

A Wheeler Park Christmas

Blood Ties

Healing Hands

Wishful Thinking

Smoke and Mirrors (January 2022)

* * *

MISS PRIMM'S ACADEMY FOR WAYWARD
WITCHES*

(Fantasy/Academy Romance)

Misspelled

Dispelled

Expelled

* * *

PROJECT DEMON HUNTERS*

(Paranormal Romance)

Unquiet Souls

Unbound Spirits

Unholy Ground

Unseen Voices

Unmarked Graves

Unbroken Vows

* * *

THE DEVIL YOU KNOW*

(Paranormal Romance)

Sympathy for the Devil

Charmed, I'm Sure

A Wing and a Prayer

* * *

THE WITCHES OF CANYON ROAD*

(Paranormal Romance)

Hidden Gifts

Darker Paths

Mysterious Ways

A Canyon Road Christmas

Demon Born

An Ill Wind

Higher Ground

Haunted Hearts

* * *

THE WITCHES OF CLEOPATRA HILL*

(Paranormal Romance)

Darkangel

Darknight

Darkmoon

Sympathetic Magic

Protector

Spellbound

A Cleopatra Hill Christmas

Impractical Magic

Strange Magic

The Arrangement

Defender

Bad Blood

Deep Magic

Darktide

* * *

THE DJINN WARS*

(Paranormal Romance)

Chosen

Taken

Fallen

Broken

Forsaken

Forbidden

Awoken

Illuminated

Stolen

Forgotten

Driven

Unspoken

* * *

THE WATCHERS TRILOGY*

(Paranormal Romance)

Falling Dark

Dead of Night

Rising Dawn

* * *

THE SEDONA FILES*

(Paranormal Romance)

Bad Vibrations

Desert Hearts

Angel Fire

Star Crossed

Falling Angels

Enemy Mine

* * *

TALES OF THE LATTER KINGDOMS*

(Fantasy Romance)

All Fall Down

Dragon Rose

Binding Spell

Ashes of Roses

One Thousand Nights

Threads of Gold

The Wolf of Harrow Hall

Moon Dance

The Song of the Thrush

* * *

THE GAIAN CONSORTIUM SERIES*

(Science Fiction Romance)

Beast (free prequel novella)

Blood Will Tell

Breath of Life

The Gaia Gambit

The Mandala Maneuver

The Titan Trap

The Zhore Deception

The Refugee Ruse

* * *

STANDALONE TITLES

Hearts on Fire

Taking Dictation

Golden Heart

Night Music: A Modern Reimagining of The Phantom
of the Opera

Ghost Dance: A Sequel to Gaston Leroux's The
Phantom of the Opera

Flight Before Christmas

* Indicates a completed series

ABOUT THE AUTHOR

USA Today bestselling author Christine Pope has been writing stories ever since she commandeered her family's Smith-Corona typewriter back in grade school. Her work includes paranormal romance, fantasy romance, and science fiction/space opera romance. She makes her home in New Mexico.

Christine Pope on the Web:
www.christinepope.com

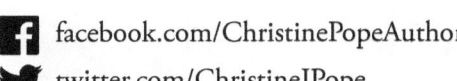

facebook.com/ChristinePopeAuthor
twitter.com/ChristineJPope
pinterest.com/ChristineJPope